THE
LAST KING

Also by Lou Paduano

The Greystone Saga

Signs of Portents

Tales from Portents

The Medusa Coin

Pathways in the Dark

A Circle of Shadows

Greystone-in-Training

Hammer and Anvil

The Gifts of Kali

The Final Gauntlet

Greystone Standalone

Army in the Obelisk

The DSA

Season One

The Clearing

Promethean

The Bridge

Spectral Advocate

Dark Impulses

Broken Loyalties

Season Two

The Wellspring

Foundations

The Missing

Cracked Chrysalis

Secret Histories

Terminal Point

THE LAST KING

A Greystone Adventure

Lou Paduano

Eleven Ten Publishing LLC

GRAND ISLAND, NEW YORK

Eleven Ten Publishing LLC
282 Fareway Lane
Grand Island, NY 14072

Printed in the United States of America
Cover art design by GetCovers

First edition published 2025

Library of Congress Cataloguing in Publication Data
Paduano, Lou
The Last King / Lou Paduano

LCCN: 2024924375
ISBN-13: 978-1-944965-57-0 (hardcover)
ISBN-13: 978-1-944965-56-3 (paperback)
ISBN-13: 978-1-944965-55-6 (eBook)

To Soriya and Loren,
for making this one so much fun.

CHAPTER ONE

The work never ended. Another page flipped under the calloused fingers of Greg Loren, his bleary eyes barely taking in the information on the page. The lamplight offered little in the way of illumination for the crammed office space. Boxes of indexed and cataloged cases rested on either side of him. All waited for his review.

Instead of the usual sounds of parading officers and boisterous detectives, quiet dominated the building. The deep hum of the Central Precinct was far away from Loren's current position—tucked in tight at a desk in what had once been the Sixth Precinct in Portents.

When the station moved north with the growing population of Venture Cove, the former location turned into an archive and storage facility known commonly as the Annex.

The place was a warehouse of paperwork. Hundreds of cold cases resided within its abandoned holding cells and interrogation rooms. They were slightly less full thanks to Loren, who had taken his fair share to an unoccupied office near the front of the building.

His reassignment was punishment, though for what, Loren no longer recalled. It had involved Mathers, of course. The day-shift captain despised Loren. Whether it had been a slight against procedure, the man's style of dress, or Mathers' mother, it mattered little to Loren. He never could hold back against the man, and he cared even less about the reprimand against him.

Most entered the former precinct with heads down and little ambition. Loren, though, took to the cold cases like a kid hunting for treasure. Some files dated back decades, long before his arrival to the city. Those on his lengthy list required a thorough review for any missing elements to the original investigation and to pass along any other recommendations to detectives in the field.

It was busy work—mindless to all but Loren. He viewed each one as an opportunity. With so many unsolved murders in Portents, there was every chance to catch a killer still on the streets and prevent another victim.

Ten days into his stint, however, Loren realized how overwhelming the numbers were against him. He felt buried beneath the weight of the past, unable to divine anything from the faded pencil marks of officers severely underpaid and too overworked to maintain their records properly.

With each page turned, Loren found another case to solve, another victim to avenge, and another murderer to catch. The day slipped away as it had so often during his time at the Annex. It wasn't until the sound of footsteps echoed in the main bullpen that Loren sat back in his chair. The clock over the door read 10:13. The irritated face of Trevor Richmond cemented the late hour.

"Go home, Loren." Trevor fixed his hat on his head. A gaunt figure in his mid-fifties, Trevor had become a regular at the Annex of late. Retirement was on the horizon for him, and everyone knew it. He needed only a few more months to reach his full pension before being able to walk out the doors and never look back.

"I will," Loren replied. His neck popped when he peered up at the ceiling. His back screamed for the same relief, but he kept to the chair.

Trevor leaned along the door, arms crossed. "The Annex might be punishment, but it's not supposed to be torture."

He saw the work as that and nothing else. Loren didn't know how to let any of it go.

"I'll try to keep that in mind," Loren said.

Trevor waited for Loren to surrender to the late hour. Loren continued to hold firm to the file before him until Trevor sighed. "Everyone else is long gone. Lock up for me?"

Loren nodded. "Sure."

The man grumbled, "If you leave, that is."

"Can't, if you keep this up."

Trevor nodded, then slipped on his jacket. "Night, Loren."

Heavy footfalls carried the man away from the office toward the double front doors. The aging wood crashed back into place with his departure and silence returned to the Annex.

Loren glanced at the clock once more. His eyes struggled to stay focused, but he fought through the fatigue. He pulled closer to the desk, hands caressing the forensic evidence list on the top sheet of the file.

The case had been bothering him for hours. To everyone else, it was simply another murder. For Loren, the case was a puzzle to unlock if only he could find the right clue, the right cipher to decode the history unveiling before him. Loren pawed through the file feverishly to find meaning in the crime's chaos.

"What am I missing?" Loren muttered under his breath. He attempted to stifle a yawn, only to have it repeat on him louder. The long night hit him again and his eyes fell on the empty mug resting on the corner of the desk. "Coffee. That's what I'm missing."

Standing, his back joined a chorus with his ankles and knees. He couldn't remember the last time he stood, let alone took a few steps. The work consumed him, ate him whole, and he let it.

The bullpen no longer contained most of the furniture it once held. Most had been transferred with the rest of the population up to the new Sixth. Some desks remained, covered with thick painting tarps. Of those still exposed to the light of the room, the vast majority were rickety old wood, including the staging table along the far wall where the coffee machine sat.

It was the only modern appliance left in the place. Loren poured what remained of the pot, thankful the burner had kept the liquid lukewarm.

As he moved for his office and the waiting case, the front doors to the Annex burst open. Loren paused, lowering his coffee to the table. His other hand edged for his service weapon.

"Hello?"

He expected Trevor, only to find a pale man with long

brown hair and a thick beard staggering into the building. The man clutched tight to his side. Blood stained his shirt.

"Hey, are you all—"

In answer to his unfinished question, the man collapsed.

"Okay," Loren said, rushing across the room. "Definitely not all right."

Loren reached for the man's side where his hand covered the torn sections of cloth from his shirt. The wounded man's other hand snatched Loren's wrist and pulled him close.

"Saw the light on," he breathed, each word a strain. "Had to try."

"Just hold on," Loren said. "I'll call—"

The man squeezed tighter. "No. Too late."

"It's not. I can—"

Tears stung the man's eyes. Blood seeped from his parted lips. A pool formed beneath his dying frame. Loren's reassuring words fell to silence.

"I was a fool. Strayed too far," the man said, his breathing erratic. "The king. The king is in danger."

"King?" Loren asked. "What—"

"You have to warn him," the dying man pleaded. "The darkness is here. It is coming for him."

His right hand let go of his gaping wound. He reached for his left wrist where a silver bracelet shone beneath the Annex's overhead lights. He struggled to pull it loose.

Loren noticed the strain on his face and tried to stop him. "Hey. It's okay. Don't—"

"I—"

The hand fell away. It slapped the tile and failed to rise again. So did the man's chest as a final breath exhaled. The tear-stained eyes stared at Loren, lost to the world.

Loren fell back, blinking hard. He looked the man over, attempting to absorb every detail. Loren's gaze fell upon the bracelet once more and he leaned over the dead man.

"What were you trying to show me?" Loren slipped the bracelet from the man's body. He stared at it, curious. There were no designs or engravings of any kind. "It's just a bracelet. Why would you—"

The man before him changed. In an instant, his entire form shifted and grew in stature. Fur replaced skin. A tail spread between his legs, a tuft of hair at the end. The man disappeared and the form of an eight-foot-tall lion took his place. Tear-stained eyes of gold remained, as did the gaping wound along his abdomen.

Loren ran his hand along his chin, the bracelet dangling between his fingers. "It's going to be one of those nights, isn't it?"

CHAPTER TWO

Lives were in danger. It was the only thought that carried Soriya Greystone down the subway tracks north from downtown Portents. The night had barely begun for her and already a threat had come to light, one she needed to put down quickly.

"See anything?"

"They can't be much farther." Mentor ran ahead, his cloak billowing behind him.

"We're coming to the coves," Soriya said, surprised at the distance traveled.

Only minutes earlier, they'd stumbled upon a pack of goblins raiding a sparsely populated subway platform on the C Line. The monsters cheered with each purse stolen and wallet palmed, spreading their mischief and violence with every patron knocked aside and laid low in their exuberance.

At Soriya's arrival, the goblins took to the shadows of the subway tunnel. In the dark beneath the city, they had thought themselves safe. Soriya and Mentor proved undeterred. With the light of the coves ahead, and the shift to an elevated rail system, Soriya worried who would be next on the goblins' hit list for the night.

Mentor said nothing, racing ahead of her for the moonlit city. As Soriya started to join him at the incline toward the surface, she paused.

The distant sound of hammering echoed around her. The beat was rhythmic, as if carried out by more than one individual.

"Do you hear that, Mentor?"

Mentor stopped at the mouth of the tunnel and looked back

at her. "They went this way, Soriya. We should—"

She held up her hand. "I'll be right there."

The sound drew her in. At the left-hand wall, she climbed off the tracks to the small ledge that ran the length of the line. The hammering grew louder. Small picks, like chisels against stone, joined the chorus. Her hand grazed the wall until her fingers slipped off the side of an arched opening.

"There's something here," Soriya called out. "A tunnel."

She gazed inside, unable to contain her curiosity. No light was seen within. No tools scraping against rock were visible down the dismally dark corridor. Before she could take her first step inside to investigate, Mentor's voice boomed down the tunnel.

"Soriya."

She hesitated only a moment, then returned to the ledge and the situation at hand. "Coming."

Hurried steps brought her to where Mentor waited impatiently. At her approach, he sighed and turned on his heels for the streets ahead. They left the platform station to the north for the border of Venture Cove.

"Are they constructing new rail lines around here?" Soriya asked.

"In the coves?" Mentor said. "Doubtful. Why?"

"Not sure. Probably nothing." Soriya shook it off. She scanned the block for signs of life. "Where are they?"

Mentor stopped her at the intersection, pointing down the road. "Where do you think?"

Six goblins ransacked a passing group of college students. It was their own fault, really. Everyone knew the unwritten rule of Portents. When the sun went down, the city was no longer a safe place to travel. The young rarely adhered to the rules, though. Clearly out for fun, running into a frantic pack of mischievous mythical creatures was the last thing on their minds.

Their mistake, Soriya thought. *And now my mess to clean up.*

She couldn't let anyone suffer if she could help it. For her, the role of the Greystone—the protector of the city—was a burden she carried proudly. It wasn't a task or a duty, but a calling she gladly took up every night.

Clothes shredded beneath the claws of the goblins. They played rough, and the innocents caught in their wake screamed for help, not that it did them any good. The goblins shrieked back, tearing open purses and tossing hard-earned cash in the air like confetti at a party.

"Goblins on holiday," Soriya grumbled. "My favorite."

"This is more than the usual mischief," Mentor replied, eyeing them cautiously as the pair entered the fray. "They seem elated about something."

Soriya shook her head. She cocked her thumb toward the clear night sky. Earth's only natural satellite hung high above them—brightly shining in deep orange and full. "It's always like this during the blood moon."

"I hope you're right, little one," Mentor said. "I think there is more to it, though."

Soriya let the discussion fall away. There wasn't time for explaining poor life choices, especially when it came to goblins—that could have taken all night. Saving those caught in their wake took priority. Soriya worked to rip the goblins away from the overwhelmed students.

Claws grasped for purchase on her. Teeth hissed their dissatisfaction at the interruption. Soon, all six stood in the center of the road. Their skin was putrid and yellowed from life underground and their clothes were little more than tatters.

Jaundiced eyes gleamed at Soriya and Mentor, who attempted to shield the innocents from further harm.

"Get those people clear, Mentor," Soriya said, fists clenched before her.

"On it," her teacher answered. He maneuvered the small crowd down the block with haste.

Soriya smirked at the goblins. "Let's see how you like a little pushback."

She leaped at the closest pair of goblins. Her fists shot forward, catching each along their pointed noses. Cartilage snapped, and green blood spilled down their faces as they fell to the street. The other four goblins took a step away from their attacker. Their eyes shifted between them as they evaluated their dwindling options.

"Not fans, are you?" Soriya prepared for another assault. Her head jerked toward her teacher. "Mentor?"

No pedestrians remained on the block. Mentor stepped forward, a small stone pressed tight to his right palm. "The street is clear."

Soriya read his look and circled around the flailing goblins. They shot at her and she batted them back with each step. Every hit contained them to the center of the block, and Mentor covered the other side to box them in.

Soriya opened the hand-woven pouch at her hip and removed the Greystone tucked inside. The stone, warm to the touch, sent a wave of exhilaration through her entire body. She raised the powerful weapon. "Ready to send our friends packing?"

Fear trickled into the goblin's faces. They tried to flee, but their movements were too staggered and too slow. The Greystones lit up; identical runes glowed brightly along the surfaces.

From out of the clear night sky, thunder boomed. Streaks of lightning crackled against the moon-filled backdrop, then blasted to the earth. An array of bolts crashed along the street. The screams of the goblins were lost, and so were they. Twin scorch marks spread from the road's center, ashes littering them from those returned to their final resting place.

"Think that was all of them?"

Mentor's jaw clenched. "For now."

Soriya shook her head. "Always the optimist. Should we…"

Her question faded. Mentor's gaze fell beyond her, gray pupils staring up into the night with a curious gaze.

"I will keep watch over the city," Mentor said. "I believe you have other plans tonight."

She wheeled around. A spotlight rose from the rooftops of the coves. A single rune was displayed against the light.

Mentor cocked an eyebrow. "It appears someone is calling you."

CHAPTER THREE

Loren tucked his hands deeper into his pockets. Any deeper and they would have ripped right through the flimsy material. The stiff wind whipped around, causing him to retreat from the roof's ledge.

The spotlight was a terrible idea, but Loren had no other. There was a dead man… lion—*whatever*—in the building below him, and he needed advice on how to proceed. His nerves refused to abate no matter the amount of pacing along the Annex's roof. What he truly needed was a cigarette, but those days were long gone. Instead, he chewed hard on a thin strip of mango-strawberry gum.

Filthy habit.

Quiet curses rose as the top of the hour approached. "Come on already." He glanced around, worried about who might show up and how he would explain the use of the emergency spotlight. "I'm going to get fired for this. Where are you?"

"Right here."

Loren spun around. Gravel kicked up beneath his well-worn sneakers. Soriya stood on the ledge. She wore a violet shirt underneath her leather jacket and ripped jeans. Her method of arrival, the pink ribbon on her left arm, retracted and came to rest at her side.

"Dammit, Soriya," Loren seethed. "You scared the hell out of me."

His scolding did little to diminish her smile. Soriya circled the spotlight. Her head nodded at the image taped on the bulb. "Hope, Loren? That's unlike you."

He pulled the switch for the spotlight down as he stared at her in confusion. "Hope?"

"The symbol," Soriya said. "Sowilo, right? It stands for—"

"It's a lightning bolt," Loren admitted, removing the hastily constructed image from the spotlight. He crumbled it between his hands. "I saw a pair not that long ago and thought... that was you, right?"

She said nothing, watching his flustered act carry him from the roof's edge for the access door to the station. She always enjoyed how he floundered when it came to their work together.

"What do you want from me, Soriya? It's not like I can call you."

"Where would the fun be in that?"

He sighed. Holding the door open, Loren ushered her ahead. "Are you going to bust my chops all night, or are you going to ask why I reached out?"

Soriya strolled over to the open door. She eyed him carefully, then nodded. "Okay, Loren. What's up?"

The Annex remained vacant. Buzzing fluorescents offered background noise to their travels down the steps and into the bullpen. Soriya waited, though her patience thinned as they moved through the building. Loren kept his comments to a minimum, unsure where to begin.

The body rested near the front of the building. Rather than leave the deceased against the cold tile of the floor, Loren had shifted him with great care, and even greater difficulty, to a pair of covered desks.

At the sight of the body, Soriya bolted across the bullpen. She stopped shy of the desks, her sneakers skidding loudly. Slow shuffling took her around the victim, her gaze wide in amazement.

"A Shishi lion."

Loren held back a chuckle. It had taken her less than three seconds to access more information than he knew about the dead creature in the room. It always astonished him how she did it, and without blinking at the absurdity of such a scenario.

"Care to run that by me again?" Loren asked.

Soriya stopped. Fingertips caught the end of the desk and

she leaned forward. "He's a guardian lion. I've never seen one before. Very rare and almost always in pairs. Their ancestry dates back to Chinese Buddhism, but they have ties to all the major lion clans in the world."

"Because that's a thing."

"They serve royalty," Soriya continued, ignoring his sarcasm. "They're stationed at imperial palaces, government buildings, that sort of thing. Like I said, they serve royalty and typically are themselves from what I've read, dating back to the…"

"Okay, okay," Loren said, waving her down. "Let's save the history lesson for the moment."

"What is he doing here?"

Loren let out a long breath. "Not much, anymore."

Soriya continued her delicate examination. When she reached the open wound along the lion's right side, she stopped. "This cut…"

"Let me guess. It's not from a human weapon, right?"

Soriya slowly nodded. Her focus remained on the wound. Green pus bubbled along the surface and ran in thin drips along the side of the tarp.

Loren inched closer. "Listen, Soriya. If someone shows up, I don't know how I'm going to explain this. The smell alone—"

"Do you have any tools?" she asked, unconcerned about human problems like explaining to your bosses why there was a dead lion in the workplace.

"No," Loren said. "It's some kind of pus, isn't it? At least, that's what it looks like to me. Ronne would know more. Not that I want to call her in on this. I can't imagine the nightmare that would be. Like I'm not in enough trouble as it is."

Soriya ran her thumb over her fingers, working up her nerve. Then she stuck her hand into the festering wound. Squishing sounds accompanied her examination.

Loren winced with each one. "What could have done this? Any thoughts, other than, ew?"

Her hand pulled away from the lion's wound. Green discharge fell in glops to the floor. She wiped the remaining fluid along her jeans.

"I don't know, Loren." Between her thumb and index finger,

Soriya held a small globe. "But this isn't pus. It's an egg."

"An egg?"

"And it wasn't alone."

The egg in her grasp rippled under her touch. In a manner of seconds, it doubled in size. Surprised, Soriya dropped it, and the egg crashed to the floor. It bounced upon impact before settling against the leg of the desk.

The strange spore continued to grow, and a shape took form within the translucent goop of the shell. The shell hardened when it reached a foot in diameter.

"What in the world?"

Loren took a step forward, then reeled away when the shell cracked. From within, a creature burst forth. It bore a large head with sharp teeth that escaped from its jawline. Scales dominating its body made it appear snake-like, but with stubby arms and legs formed along the sides.

"What is—"

Soriya grabbed Loren by the arm and pulled him away. "Keep back."

"Why? What—"

Dozens of eggs popped free from their prison within the gaping wound of the dead lion. Their growth accelerated as they fell so that when they hit the tile, the shells had already hardened and started to crack.

The first creature looked on as more of its brethren joined it.

Loren stood stock-still, unable to tear himself away from the strange sight. Soriya, though, kept her fists clenched.

"They're kind of cute, don't you think?"

"Loren…"

After the eggs finished hatching, the creatures turned to the pair. Their jaws snapped open to reveal a maw of jagged teeth—hungry for dinner.

"Okay," Loren said. "Maybe not so cute after all."

CHAPTER FOUR

Soriya continued to edge Loren away from the hatched eggs. The creatures gnashed their teeth, batting at each other like they were siblings fighting over their favorite toys.

She hated having Loren at her side in situations like this. There were moments to share, those where she maintained some knowledge of what they were dealing with. With the unknown, all she could do was keep him safe and even that was no longer a guarantee.

"They look like snakes. Like snake-kids?" Loren commented, unable to peel his eyes away from them.

The horde of creatures peered around anxiously, then settled on the corpse that had once served as their host. Opening wide, the group jumped at the dead lion. In a manner of seconds, the corpse was gone, consumed by the chomping teeth of the creatures. Fur, flesh, and bones vanished along with the synthetic fibers of his clothes. So did the blood-soaked tarp covering the twin desks.

Loren's eyes widened. "Make that starving snake-kids."

Their hunger failed to stop with the dead lion. Having tasted his flesh, each of the creatures turned to a new goal. Their bodies continued to grow until settling in at four-feet tall. Small claws spread from their fingers and toes. Hisses erupted as they spread out in search of their next meal.

When all eyes fell upon Loren and Soriya, both knew what came next: dessert.

"You said this place was empty?" Soriya asked, a hand to Loren's chest to back him toward the exit.

Loren couldn't even look at her. "Yeah."

"Good." She spun around and snatched his hand. "Come on."

He was lifted off his feet for a second, then joined her. "What are we going to do?"

"Only thing we can," Soriya replied. "Run."

The reptilian children bounded toward them. Screams of anticipation filled the bullpen. The sound of their jaws snapping at every piece of furniture caught between them and their next meal sounded like a buzz-saw slicing through sheets of wood.

Loren glanced back and nearly fell over. "Run?"

Soriya pulled him along. The front doors to the Annex were just out of reach. "I don't know what this is, Loren. I can't risk your life."

Entire desks disappeared in the feeding frenzy. Nails and screws pinged on the tile, then rolled away, the only survivors of the meal. The children ate all in sight in their pursuit of the pair at the front doors. Some took to the floor, splitting open the tile only to fall between the beams. They popped out closer to the exit and their targets.

Soriya opened the door, holding it for Loren.

He hesitated, another glance back in terror. "You're worried about me?"

"Aren't you?"

"Well, yeah."

Soriya yanked on his wrist until he crossed the threshold. The second he was outside the building, she slammed the doors shut.

"What is that going to do?" Loren said.

Soriya grimaced. "I'm working on it."

She left him at the handles, and he took hold. The entire frame shook with the arrival of the children. They beat against the slabs of wood. The sound of their eating continued to surround Soriya, and she wondered what might be distracting them from taking down the doors.

Grateful for the momentary reprieve, Soriya shot down the stairs. The Greystone was back in her hand and she channeled her will into the obol.

Strength coursed through her. Utilizing her newfound might, Soriya grabbed the metal railing to the right of the stoop and pulled. Anchors split under the pressure and the entire rail soared loose. Soriya carried it up the steps. Jamming it through the handles of the door, Soriya twisted the railing around like a pretzel.

Loren backed away. The doors shifted with each assault by the creatures inside, but they held tight thanks to the improvised lock.

"That should hold them," Soriya said. "For a bit, at any rate."

Loren scanned the street. "The place should be vacant for the rest of the night. Should be."

The slamming increased on the other side of the door. Soriya tucked the Greystone away and placed her hands on the slabs to offer more support. Slight cuts formed along the bottom half of the doors. The kids were working their way through.

"Tell me more about the lion, Loren."

"Like what?"

"He must have said something—mentioned something— that might give me a clue about what we're dealing with."

Loren rubbed the back of his neck. "I'm used to you having all the answers."

"I'm not an encyclopedia, Loren," Soriya snapped. "What do you know?"

Loren joined her at the door to add his strength to their crumbling barricade. "He mentioned a king. Sounded like he was protecting him."

"Yes," Soriya grumbled through clenched jaw. "Shishi are notorious guardians. I said that."

"Don't be snippy."

"Loren."

He closed his eyes, fighting against the sound of the shattering door and the wood chips flying free as the chomping jaws inched closer to escaping.

His eyes snapped open, brighter than before. "He said the darkness was coming for the king."

Soriya rolled her eyes. "Where can we find the king?" A blank stare was his only reply. "Did he give a name? An address? Anything useful?"

"I don't… He didn't tell me." Loren fell back a step. His hand shot up and he snapped his fingers. Reaching behind him, he removed a small black billfold from his jacket pocket. "I did manage to hang onto this."

Soriya blinked hard. "He was carrying a wallet?"

Loren flipped it open. The victim's license fell into his hand. "There's an address listed here. It's not far." He held it out to her. "Is that enough of a start for you?"

CHAPTER FIVE

The pair raced down the stoop of the repurposed police station. Minor arguments cropped up between them, the male pointing back to the shattering doors with some concern. The female—clearly in charge—kept him moving down the block until the pair disappeared completely.

The block emptied with their departure. Streetlights, once bright to combat the darkness of the night, flickered and faded. The moonlight dimmed as if obstructed by some unseen force as shadows took over the entire area.

They streamed out of every alleyway and up from the sewers. Strands of obsidian snaked from beneath the parked cars on the adjacent blocks and from behind bus stop overhangs and newspaper boxes. Each one lingered in the air, as if sniffing the very breath of the city. They trailed the departing pair to the first intersection, then hesitated to follow further.

The pair had their role to play in what was to come. But a greater need existed at the moment. The shadows felt the presence within the precinct building. The call of their children was too much to ignore.

Strands of shadow, the deep darkness of the night, washed back to the precinct in a wave. With every inch gained, the separate pieces bonded with their neighbors. They took form in the street at the base of the stoop. Eyes of pure black and scales to match stepped clear of the darkness. Hovered, though, was more appropriate as the feet of the figure never touched solid ground. The hiss of his tongue announced his arrival to the beings locked away in the building.

Ur walked the world once more.

It had been far too long. For millennia, Ur had remained locked away—chained in a darkness that continued to trail his every movement. The shadows were his cloak, but they were also his guide in the world—this ripe and rich place begging for change… begging for him.

He had recognized the shift in the air of his void prison. From out of the darkness, there was the twinkling of hope again. It was all he'd sought in his existence, a place of his own, where darkness reigned and light was forsaken, the way he had always been forsaken.

The moment the gates had opened, Ur had stepped through. He had seized his destiny and would not depart again. Nothing would stand in his way.

No. *Their* way.

He was no longer alone. Strands of darkness ripped away the twisted railing from the handles and the doors swung open. His children rushed from the building, surrounding him with the exuberance of youth. They nipped at the shadows, unable to take hold of his essence. When they attempted to do the same to him, Ur's shadow cloak slapped them away.

Slowly, they came to realize his presence and their role. Heads bowed as a calm fell over them.

Ur spread his arms and smiled. "Welcome to the world, my children."

His shadows wrapped around them tenderly. As he studied them, his eyes flitted inside the building. The fallen lion was gone, but the stench of death remained pungent.

Ur's smile grew wider and more insidious. The guardian had served his purpose. Ur had been lucky enough to locate the mangy beast. It had been completing mundane tasks, never once considering the danger. The guardian had grown soft and complacent. It had made the killing almost a mercy. One Ur sought to give to the rest of the world in time.

Mutterings rose from the hatchlings. His children were a curious lot, and he understood their snaps and their moans immediately.

"It has been too long," Ur said, his voice reverberating

through the darkness that was his being. "The protections have finally faded. After so long, we have a foothold here once more. However, our time is limited."

The snapping of jaws grew. Their bellies roared, ravenous for the meal ahead. "Yes, my children. Once the talisman is mine, this world will be your playground. It will be an endless bounty for you to feast upon."

Eyes widened with pleasure. Their needs were simple. Ur pointed the way, and the shadows stretched far to the east toward the pair who had so recently departed.

"Follow them," Ur commanded. "Find the talisman. Then, at long last, our darkness will reign."

The children raced ahead, chomping at the air and the scent of their prey. Ur fell back into his shadows. They spread wide and waited.

His time was coming. It was all but inevitable.

CHAPTER SIX

Loren held his phone in the air. Another block faded behind them, the darkness somehow thicker despite the blood moon overhead. He squinted at the screen, then scanned the surrounding area. Nothing appeared familiar.

"Wait," he said, holding up Soriya. "Are we supposed to go west or east on Hickman?"

Soriya huffed. The delay brought out her impatience. She snatched the phone from him and pointed as the route illuminated. "How do you not know where you're going in this city, Loren?"

He shrugged. "Too busy running from monsters."

"Cute," Soriya replied. She waved him ahead, taking over the phone and the lead. "It's this way."

They started east. Hurried steps carried them across residential neighborhoods. No lights beamed from the homes. No sounds rose through closed windows and drawn curtains. The city was theirs for the duration. It made Loren feel more isolated.

He continued to look back. He couldn't help it. All Loren pictured with each rushing step into the Portents night was the sight of sharpened teeth. All he heard was the gnashing of those teeth on anything or anyone they came upon. A pit formed in his stomach. His guilt trailed his every thought until it spilled out of him.

"We shouldn't have left those things," he said, catching up with the long gait of his companion. "Who knows the damage they might do?"

"No choice," Soriya said without looking. She was busy monitoring the numbers on the passing properties. Another block vanished behind them.

"Your stone thing—"

Soriya halted, a hand raised before him. "The Greystone isn't always the answer."

The comment surprised him. Their time together had certainly proved differently. Whenever they had been backed into a corner, whether it was by crazed masked killers or vengeful gremlins, the stone had always come through in the end.

"Why not?" he asked. "I've seen you do some incredible things with that stone. Why didn't you—"

"I've never seen anything like those snakes before, Loren," Soriya answered. "If I used the Greystone on them without knowing what they can do or what they really are? I could have made the situation worse."

Loren let the words settle between them. A slight nod escaped him and he resumed walking.

"Okay." Her maturity impressed him. He wondered when his own would catch up. "Sorry I pushed."

"It's fine," she said. "It wouldn't have mattered anyway if I had taken care of those things or not. They clearly didn't kill the lion. Something else did. Something else implanted them in their victim."

Loren shook his head, trying to banish the image from his mind. Hands gently ran down his sides, hoping not to find any entry points. "So, figuring out who this king is will hopefully tell us what's going on?"

"Exactly."

"A king, though?" Loren asked in disbelief. "In this day and age?"

"Not a king in the traditional sense, Loren."

"I assumed," he muttered. Loren knew enough about Portents to realize tradition went out the window in most, if not all, situations.

Soriya's pace increased as they turned south down Siegel. "Kings once controlled the fates of whole worlds. Entire planes of existence lived or died with the passing of their ruler. These weren't malevolent beings, but genuine leaders—walking spirits of good, protecting all from the evil in the dark."

"What happened to them?"

"They left," she said, distant eyes gazing upward at the stars. "One by one, they faded with the passage of time. If one is here…"

Loren waited for more, but nothing came. Soriya had stopped short of a two-story brick structure at the end of the block of Siegel and Binder. The exterior appeared chipped and cracked from age. The doorknocker—that of a lion's head—was tarnished and peeled.

"This is the place," she said.

Soriya tossed the phone to Loren. The screen showed the address found in the dead lion's wallet. It seemed strange to be standing at the residence of such a creature—hidden among so many other people. Loren wondered how long the poor soul had remained a secret from his neighbors, and how many others lived in the same situation day-in and day-out within the confines of Portents.

He pocketed his phone and stepped up to the front of the home. He attempted to peer through the windows for signs of life inside, but thick curtains blocked his view. When he turned toward the front door, Soriya was already there with her hand on the knob.

"Let's go, Loren."

"Maybe we should knock." She wrenched the door open from the frame before Loren could reach her. "Soriya…"

Standing at the threshold, Loren hesitated. Shadows dominated the wide foyer, and the only form he made out was Soriya in the room.

"We didn't need to break in," Loren whispered. "We could have done this differently."

"That would have been advisable," a voice snarled from behind them. Both wheeled around, but not before twin paws shoved them deeper into the home.

The door slammed shut, cutting off any light to the room. Loren searched madly for their attacker, blinking hard to adjust to the dark. Shifting feet, barely audible against the carpet, gave him the general vicinity of an enormous figure. It wasn't until a tail brushed against a nearby curtain and brought in streams of moonlight that Loren truly saw the lion.

Claws extended from his immense paws. The lion stood over eight-feet-tall, definitely stronger and more built than the victim Loren had encountered earlier in the night. The beast appeared to want nothing more than their blood.

"Holy…" Loren muttered. He was stuck in place, locked on the imposing creature.

Soriya, of course, knew better than to stand still in the face of such an adversary. She leaped toward Loren as the lion charged at them.

"Loren, get down!"

She tackled him hard to the ground, the carpet doing little to cushion the impact. Sharp, hooked nails swiped over them, a killing stroke if Loren had to guess. This thing wasn't playing around.

Soriya rolled off Loren, then kicked out at the creature. He howled as her foot connected with the back of his leg. Recovering quickly, he swung out, but Soriya was already on her feet and moving.

"Back off, kitty."

"You dare enter this holy place without invitation?" the lion snarled. "You shall pay for that error in judgment."

Soriya cocked her fist back. "Not without a fight."

A right cross connected with the lion's mane. He failed to budge from the blow. His paw caught her in the chest and she staggered back a step. Before she could react, the lion spun around. His tail wrapped around her arm and lifted her from the ground. She crashed in a heap near the front door.

Wiping dabs of saliva from her lips, Soriya bounded back into the fray. They traded blow for blow, constantly maneuvering against each other's strikes for a better opportunity.

Loren, though, stood alone on the far side of the room. Behind him were twin pocket doors, and he leaned along the side of the frame. From his pocket, he pulled out the victim's silver bracelet, trying to remember why they had come.

"Soriya, we don't—"

"I've got this, Loren," she shot back as she ducked a sweep of the lion's paw.

Loren stepped toward them, a hand in the air. "But we could—"

"Loren!" Soriya shouted over the growl of her assailant.

"It's just…" Loren sighed. He held the bracelet before him.

The moonlight caught the bright finish of the jewelry. The glare passed over the lion's eyes and he attempted to shield them while blocking Soriya's roundabout kick. He took the strike to the cheek, then tossed her aside, his gaze still locked on the bracelet.

"Where did you get that?" he roared at Loren.

"I—"

The lion charged. His roar echoed through the room, and his paws slapped at the carpet as he readied for the kill. Loren, so caught up in the imminent death in front of him, failed to notice the sudden breeze behind him.

The pocket doors had opened and a lanky figure stood at Loren's side. His hand lifted the bracelet from Loren's grip.

"Idris, stop," the man said, his tone soft but the command clear.

Loren turned. A soft glow of white surrounded the man. He bore a thick, dark beard and a cloak of green decorated in gold trim. A crown rested upon his head. The man caressed the bracelet before him, a treasured item.

"Barnabas has fallen," the man said.

The lion—Idris—stopped short of Loren. He took to his knee and raised a fist to his chest. "My lord."

Soriya's chest heaved from the fight. Her fists remained raised, ready for more.

The others, however, looked them over. The lord of the home beamed at the intruders and waved them to the parlor in the next room.

"It appears we have much to discuss."

CHAPTER SEVEN

The parlor offered a more intimate setting. Twin couches sat facing each other, with a single rocking chair at the head of the room. Behind the chair hung a drabsha, the white sheath draped with care around two thick boughs of olive wood. Seven branches of a white flowering plant—myrtle—attached the olive wood together and rose from the back.

Bookshelves wrapped around the walls to the right and left of the centerpiece. There were religious texts, their names unmarked along the spine except for the barest of iconography. A grandfather clock of gold rested in one corner; it slowly ticked away the midnight hour.

Idris helped keep the beat of the clock. His pacing trailed behind the empty couch and around his king's position at the head of the room. With each uncomfortable glance, Soriya felt her blood run red hot. She tried to stand, only to be stopped with a firm hand by Loren, accompanied by a sharp glare.

The lion broke the silence in a thundering voice. "What happened to Barnabas?"

"He… He was killed. By what, we don't know." Loren took a breath and leaned forward. Idris waited for more; the explanation offered nothing in the way of peace. Unfortunately, they had little information to share with the bereaved. Loren, instead, turned to the king. "He said the darkness was coming. For you."

The king took the words and let them linger in the room's silence. Then he offered a stoic nod and said a single word.

"Ur."

Soriya jumped to her feet. "Ur?"

"You know what this is, Soriya?" Loren asked.

Soriya pushed past him, a finger toward the king. "That means you're—"

The lord of the house smiled. It wasn't in arrogance or even in jest. The gesture, a slight tip of the lips on both sides, was the most honest smile Soriya had ever seen.

"I have gone by many names from many followers," he said in his soft voice. "You may call me Aram."

Loren huffed loudly. He slapped his knees hard and shook his head. "Nope."

"Loren," Soriya murmured. She read the look on his face well. For all the ordeals they had endured together, Loren hated playing the ignorant fool. Every name, every utterance, passed by him without a single point of reference. When it came to their work, it had always led to frustration, especially when lives were at stake.

"I'm sorry, your lordship, or whatever I'm supposed to call you."

"You will address him as—"

"Aram will suffice," the king interjected, over the snarl of his guardian.

"I'm a cop," Loren continued. "This world? None of this is what I'm built for. So, I need someone in this room to say something I can understand. I need that to happen right now."

Soriya bit back her response. His anger matched her own, but for an entirely different reason. Where she finally saw the reason behind the night's events, Loren remained lost.

Aram inched forward, a hand on the armrest of his chair. It seemed to hold him steady, his body shivering with the movement. "Ur is a powerful demon of the underworld. He has been locked in the darkness for ages—kept at bay. By this."

Reaching into his cloak, Aram returned with a circular talisman. It was gold with four images embossed on the surface. At the center walked a lion, tall and proud. A wasp and a scorpion flanked the image. A snake, with eyes of the deepest black, circled the entire trio.

"What is it?" Loren asked.

"It is called the skandola," Aram answered.

"It's supposed to ward off evil," Soriya said. Aram accepted the response, settling back in his chair. "People keep them in their homes to protect their loved ones."

"This is the original," Aram said. "It carries a much wider reach. Or it did."

Loren watched closely as the king returned the skandola to his cloak. "What's changed?"

"The king has shared enough," Idris growled. His paws encircled his master's chair, ever the protector, even in a civilized discussion.

The king's hand fell upon the lion's paw. "Idris."

"I will take care of Ur and protect you for the rite," Idris said, his tone much more refined when addressing Aram.

"They can help." The king motioned to his guests.

"We will." Soriya's statement caused Loren to flinch back in surprise.

His arms crossed his chest. "Help with what, exactly?"

Soriya let out a deep breath. She sat on the edge of the couch. "Aram is dying. That's why Ur is here now. The protection is fading."

"It will continue to fade until my passing," Aram confirmed.

Loren glanced around the room. "What can we do?"

Aram stood. He stumbled a little to the left, but caught himself against the chair. Idris was at the king's side for support, though Aram waved him off.

"My tomb waits for us," Aram said. "When I pass beyond its border, the skandola will be renewed. Light will return to the world and Ur will be banished back to the underworld."

Idris shook his head. Any thought of the king's death clearly pained him, almost as much as the loss of his brother-in-arms. Instead of rage, though, only sadness rested in his golden eyes.

"The preparations are nearly complete," Idris said, though the words lacked any sense of confidence. "If only we hadn't delayed for so long. I should have —"

"Recriminations will get us nowhere, my friend." Aram's smile returned to his face. "What will be, will be. But I don't believe we can wait here any longer." Brilliant eyes of blue looked to Soriya. "Do you?"

"No," she said. Loren wrung his hands, clearly unsettled by the entire affair. Still, there was only one answer, and she knew better than to hold it back from those in need. "No, I don't think we can."

CHAPTER EIGHT

Idris and Aram met in the corner of the room. The latter appeared depleted from the long night. His shoulders slumped and the light that glowed around him frequently dimmed to nothing before struggling to reappear. Idris attended him, carefully wrapping a heavy cloak around the king's shoulders. He handed over a small satchel, which Aram strapped to his belt for safekeeping. It jingled slightly as he shifted his weight.

The great lion wore the vestments of a warrior. Plated armor covered his chest, strapped tight over his shoulders and around his abdomen; an image of the skandola was brandished in the center. No weapons hung from his thick belt. None were needed with the strength carried by the legendary beast.

His words with the king were lost on Loren, but the conversation never turned heated. Concern was the watchword of the night, especially from Idris, who clearly desired nothing more than to take care of the threat against his master.

Soriya appeared in the same boat. As she leaned along the door frame, her fingers needled along the wood. Her toes tapped against the carpet where she stood. Staying in place had never been her strong suit, but at least she was prepared for what came next—or seemed to be, anyway.

Loren knew nothing, not about the threat—despite the history lesson given—or about how they could actually handle a demon or whatever the hell Ur really was. His night spun completely out of his control, as it always did when Soriya became involved.

Whose fault is that? He had been the one to bring her in, requiring the advice of the Greystone. What good had it done? Information continued to elude him.

His frustration rose. Loren ran his hands over his pant legs as sweat filled his palms. Unable to handle the wait any longer, Loren jumped to his feet and moved for the pocket doors.

"Got a second, Soriya?" he asked, nodding to the open foyer.

She indicated the pair within the parlor, who continued to prepare. "Loren, we need to—"

"A second," Loren repeated with a stern glare. "Over here."

She pushed from the wall and Loren closed the parlor doors. He led her to the far side of the foyer. Slick fingers ran through his hair to massage his scalp. He tried to slow his racing heart and spinning thoughts.

He failed. "What the hell are we talking about here?"

The words crashed into Soriya, throwing her off guard. She blinked hard, then leaned close to keep her volume low. "You heard what Aram said."

"I heard about a token with the power to banish darkness from the world."

Soriya nodded. "That's right."

"We're just going with that?" Loren snapped in disbelief. His eyes felt like they might explode from his skull. "No questions asked?"

"Loren—"

He threw his hands into the air. Swift pacing carried him around the room, though it did little to calm him. "I know. I know we've seen some crazy crap together, but this? Kings and lions and snake things?"

"Oh, my," Soriya said. He glared at her, forcing her to shrug. "Sorry. Had to."

Loren grumbled. "I'm supposed to be solving cold cases, Soriya. Actual murderers are out there right now. In the real world."

"This is real too."

He couldn't look at her. Everything about her always complicated matters and here he was inviting the chaos into his life only to reject it at the first opportunity. His thoughts lingered on the case files on his desk and the dead who needed justice.

Then he thought of Barnabas.

A hand settled along his shoulder. Soriya squeezed lightly. "Who else will help them, Loren? Who else can?"

He had thought the same about his work. No one else cared enough to continue the manhunt on the old cases. Even his wife's death remained nothing more than a bunch of reports tucked away in a box somewhere in the Annex. They all deserved more. So did Barnabas.

Soriya didn't hesitate somehow. It didn't matter if she knew the victim or not. If there was someone in need, she was prepared to fight on their behalf. She protected everyone somehow, never asking for anything in return. He envied her resolve while cursing his own indecision.

Loren nodded slowly.

The pocket doors opened. Idris and Aram stood ready to depart, the king leaning heavily on his protector for support. Barnabas wasn't the only who needed Loren tonight.

"Where do we go?"

Idris could barely meet the question. "I have not heard yet."

"The construction was kept secret," Aram clarified. "We were to be notified when the site was completed."

Soriya wheeled toward them. "Construction?"

"What is it?"

"There were these noises earlier," she said, the thought heavy in her brown eyes. "Would this place happen to be underground?"

"Yes," Idris replied. "How did you—"

Soriya stopped him with a raised hand and smiled. "I know where we have to go."

CHAPTER NINE

Soriya took little time to describe her eventful evening. She started with the sounds heard in the subway tunnels leading from the cove to downtown Portents. Once the pack of goblins entered the colorful yarn, Loren tuned out. There was enough stress in his life without thinking about terrors he could only imagine hiding around every corner of his city. Aram, though, didn't help matters.

"We should move quickly," he said. "Ur will gain strength the more time he spends in this world."

Loren grumbled, "Of course he will. Any other good news to share?"

Idris opened the door and ushered them from the home. The night wind blew around them, a chilling reminder of the late hour. Aram stuck close to his guardian, Loren slow to move down the stairs.

Soriya squeezed his arm. "One step at a time, Loren."

"That is far enough," a voice echoed from all around them.

The group stopped at the top of the stoop. Idris still held tight to the doorknob. Loren nearly ran into the side of Soriya. His eyes were locked on the street.

The snake children spread in a wide arc across the road. Massive jaws chomped exuberantly for their next meal; saliva ran in streams from their lipless mouths.

The figure in the middle of the group kept them at bay. Or at least, he appeared to be in the middle. The voice claimed differently and seemed to emerge from every strand of shadow that surrounded the domicile.

Coalescing, the figure took hold. He bore the body of a snake, scales of deep midnight with eyes to match. A forked tongue whispered from his mouth. No sharpened fangs were necessary; his entire body was built like a weapon—with nails like small daggers at the end of his fingers and a cloak of black that snapped to attention, sharp like blades.

The familial resemblance was clear. Ur was a monster in the truest sense, and one above it all as he hovered over the street by inches.

Aram edged past the group. Slowly, he took to the stairs until he was at the curb, his hands before him and full of light.

"Ur."

Idris followed closely. His own paws were ready to strike. "You murdered my brother."

Ur stared disconcertedly at the accusation. Then a wispy grin broke through his scaly surface. "Oh, I did. He suffered greatly as I cut him down. You should have heard him beg for his life. Will you beg as well, guardian?"

The lion prepared to pounce. There was no care about the number of enemies before him, only the revenge he sought for the dead.

Aram kept him from the confrontation, a soft hand along his furry forearm. "Idris. Time stands against us."

"Yeah, well, these things aren't giving us a lot of options," Loren said.

The children of Ur shifted with their movements. As the group inched away from the home for the end of the block, the hatchlings snapped madly in the air, ready for a late-night snack. The image was enough to make Loren cover his mouth to keep from retching.

"Thoughts, Soriya?"

"Yeah," she said without looking. Her fists clenched at her sides and she took a step into the street. "Go."

"What?" Loren exclaimed.

"You know the way," she said, continuing toward the enemy. "Take them and get to the tomb."

"Not without you."

Soriya shot him a smirk. "I'll be right behind you."

For the first time in their brief association, he didn't believe her. Soriya had done nothing but try to protect him since her arrival. That remained her top priority over her own safety.

Loren stepped toward her and the fight ahead. Ur watched gleefully, the shadows shivering with anticipation. All around him, the darkness' children prepared for their feast. The reticent detective stopped himself, a curse on his lips.

"Dammit, Soriya…"

"There's no time for an argument," she said. Her walk turned into a run. "Now, go!"

Loren closed his eyes and backed away. He pulled at Idris and Aram. Both wore their worries on their faces. There was nothing any of them could do. Soriya was right. They had to leave her behind. Their task was too important—their time too limited to wait.

He pushed them down the block for the subway tunnel in the distance. "We need to move. Come on."

CHAPTER TEN

Ur was the threat, and she started with him. Launching into the air, Soriya pulled back her fist. She drove it at his grinning face, only to have it pass right through him.

She slammed into the ground, then kicked out at him. Her foot bled past his hovering form and into the very shadows of the night. Ur carried no mass, like the darkness itself kept him visible in the world.

The second she paused her attack to re-evaluate her strategy, the hatchlings surrounded her. Their jagged teeth snapped madly at her. Soriya spun around, kicking and punching out for some breathing space.

Four fell back. A lucky blow cracked the skull of another. There remained too many to handle. The die had been cast, though. Soriya had made her choice and stood by it, Greystone in hand.

There was no time for hesitation—no time for worrying about the consequences of her actions. If she failed, Loren and the others were dead. No other outcome presented itself and wouldn't.

Ur had risen.

A nighttime terror read by Mentor in the quiet candlelight of the Bypass Chamber, Soriya had always feared such a creature's return to the world. Ur, like so many other demons or gods, was an elemental force of nature, more than a creature of physical form. There was nothing to hit, nothing to subdue, and that left her cold.

Soriya wasn't left powerless, however. She squeezed the

small stone between her fingers. The surface lit up as she channeled her will into the ancient weapon.

Wind picked up. The shadows spread, pushed back from Soriya's position. Ur struggled to maintain his form. He bled into the dark rather than fight against her. The hatchlings had no escape plan. They dug their claws into the pavement without success.

Soriya edged closer, screaming as her every effort poured into the Greystone. One by one, Ur's children soared away from her. They crashed into parked cars or bounded over them for the buildings down the block. One hit the front of Aram's domicile with such force his skull caved in, and he collapsed to the ground—dead on impact.

When the light finally dimmed along the surface, Soriya fought to catch her breath. It was another downside of utilizing the stone to such a degree: her will might have seemed infinite to others, like Loren, but there was a limit to her strength. She staggered slightly before she caught herself.

The shadows reformed in the center of the road. The grin returned to the snake at the heart of the darkness. "Your strength is impressive," Ur said. "Still, you must see the futility in your task. We have been locked away for millennia. This is our time. Your world will be ours."

Soriya raced toward him. "That's not going to happen."

She held back, waiting until she passed through Ur to throw her fist out. It caught one hatchling across the face and the monster dropped where she hit it.

Four more surrounded her. Soriya leaped over the first's clumsy assault, then caught two in their chests with a blistering double-kick. They staggered back as she landed on her feet and delivered a sharp left cross to the final hatchling.

Each movement was graceful, a continuous motion that brought her to every threat in turn. She couldn't stop, not for a second; the danger never abated long enough for her to take a single breath let alone gain any kind of reprieve.

"You won't get to Aram," Soriya said between punches. "I won't let you."

In her haste to subdue the starving children, she lost sight of Ur. The shadows continued to flit around the area, dancing on the wind rather than coalescing to any semblance of the great beast.

With her back turned in attending the hatchlings, the stone bearer noted a shift in the breeze. The dark penetrated everything, swirling in an arc around her, until Ur returned. Claw-like fingers stretched out tight together as a weapon and struck.

"You have no choice in the matter." Ur's words echoed through the darkness. "Not any longer."

At the last second, Soriya twisted—more instinct than anything planned. Ur sliced through her side and she cried out from the sudden pain. As she fell, Soriya reached for the wound. It ran six inches along her right side. Her saving grace was that it wasn't terribly deep, though the blow exposed several layers of skin.

Nestled in the wound were pockets of green liquid—what Loren had mistaken for pus from Ur's previous victim. Soriya knew better, and her eyes widened with terror. She felt the liquid shifting inside… and growing.

Looming over her, Ur whispered into her ear, "My children are coming."

With that, the ancient evil stepped away. The damage had been done, and there was nothing left for him to do but wait until Soriya finished playing host to more of his offspring.

"No." Soriya fought to stand. Her legs gave way, and she crashed to her knees along the pavement. "I won't let you. I won't—"

Shadows stabbed out from the back of Ur's cloak. They wrapped tight around her arms. Lifting her from the ground, the shadows threw her away like so much garbage. Soriya skidded across the street and crashed into the side of Aram's stoop.

Ur looked back only once, satisfaction caught in the hiss of his forked tongue. "Come," he called to his children. "The king awaits."

All departed. They left Soriya in the shadows of the stoop, defeated. She clutched tight to her side, knowing her time was quickly running out.

46

CHAPTER ELEVEN

Loren rushed ahead of the group. He crossed the street, glancing in both directions. Nothing appeared familiar to him. If they had been in the Knoll, he would have at least had some understanding of their destination. Their only saving grace was the signage found on every other block denoting the subway platform into the city.

Waving the others ahead, Loren continued across Shuster. "We're close. I think."

"Good." Idris walked awkwardly beside the king. His steps were subdued, clearly unwilling to leave his charge behind. Aram struggled forward; his feet barely lifted from the pavement. His light fought to present, more and more depleted the farther they traveled in the coves.

Cutting across the field at Shuster and Broome brought the trio to the platform and the tracks beyond. No trains came through at the late hour, the place abandoned for the night. Loren stepped down to the tracks, then helped Aram do the same. Idris bounded after them and they continued toward the looming tunnel.

The lion slowed to give Aram the lead. His pace matched Loren's intentionally, and the detective took the hint. They kept the same rhythm, their steps in tune with each other. Idris glanced at Loren with increasing frequency. Loren tried not to take notice. He stared ahead and chewed loudly on the twin sticks of gum caught between his teeth.

"What is it you are doing?" Idris finally asked. "That sound… it's irritating."

"What sound?"

"Your chewing," Idris replied. "What are you eating?"

"Gum." Loren removed the pack from his pocket. "Want some?"

Idris grimaced. "A vile habit."

"Right?" Loren said in full agreement. "It's the worst."

The lion eyed his companion strangely.

Loren spit the flavorless mass into an empty wrapper. He looked for a garbage can to dump it, but found none. Sticking it inside his pocket, he felt the wad beneath his fingers and winced.

"Problem?" Idris asked, his voice full of curiosity.

"You tell me," Loren said, pulling his fingers loose from his pocket. He nodded to the king ahead of them. "How bad is he?"

Idris' head dipped to the ground. "He's fading much faster now."

"Why?" Loren asked. "He looks…"

Loren didn't know what to say. So much of his experiences with Soriya went beyond human understanding.

"Healthy?" Idris said in Loren's silence.

Loren knew the answer to that already, having been around the king for the last few hours. "I was thinking more… young? Young-ish?"

Idris nodded. A sad grin spread beneath the lion's mane. "He is far older than you can imagine. In his days, civilizations rose and fell. Entire races came into being and now lay extinct."

"So, not so young."

"No," Idris replied with a chuckle.

The sound of gravel kicking loose beneath their steps accompanied their walk. Aram stood at the shadow of the tunnel, then dipped into the darkness.

"You've been with him through it all?" Loren asked.

"Not quite," Idris said. "I was but a cub when I was chosen to serve him. Barnabas… He taught me what it meant to be a guardian. We were together for our whole lives."

"I'm sorry about your friend," Loren said. "He was incredibly brave, Idris. So are you."

Idris huffed, shucking off the compliment. "I fulfill my duty.

That is all."

Loren couldn't help but laugh. *A modest lion. Who would have thought?*

"You're kidding, right? You stand by a king. Never wavering. Never faltering. Never questioning your loyalty or your role. That's incredible. You're incredible."

Idris halted. "I find that strange coming from you."

Loren cocked an eyebrow.

The lion grinned. "You protect an entire city. The challenges in that must seem insurmountable, yet you continue to face them." He resumed their walk through the tunnel. "We both carry our tasks in everything we do. And we could not live without them."

The pile of cases flashed through Loren's thoughts. They waited for his review, hoping against hope he might find the answers that had been missing for so long. They had been meant as a punishment from Mathers, but to him, they were anything but.

"Heh." Loren rubbed at his chin. "I guess I never thought of it that way."

Idris stood a little taller at the unspoken compliment from the detective. The pair continued through the dark, surprised at the lack of light before them. For a moment, there was dread in their step and fear in their eyes, as all sight of Aram was lost.

From within the shadows, the king called, "Detective."

They raced ahead to the king's position. Aram pointed down the tunnel. As much as they knew where they were headed, they were simply wandering in the dark without Soriya to tell them where she'd heard the sound of construction in the bowels of Portents.

Loren straightened his collar and shifted ahead of his companions. "Right," he muttered, as he peered around for signs of the passage. He kept to the ledge off the right side of the tracks and ran his hands against the jagged rock.

"Soriya mentioned some kind of hammering somewhere around…" His words cut out. The jagged rock grew smoother the farther down the line he traveled until it suddenly vanished. "Here."

Idris and Aram joined him at the opening. Even with the dim glow of Aram still present, nothing could be seen in the depths of the passage. Only darkness remained before them.

"Can you see anything?" Loren asked.

"No," Idris answered.

The king pushed forward, a hand to the wall. "Darkness cannot stop us now."

Before Aram could enter the dark, Idris stopped him. The touch was gentle, the soft look to the ground a clear apology to the king.

"Allow me, my lord," he said.

"Thank you, Idris."

Loren held up the lion from taking his place at the head of the chain. "Yeah, thanks, big guy. But I think I should take the lead here."

"Why?"

Loren pulled the lighter from his pocket—his ever-present reminder to the habit he still so desperately craved—and flicked it on. A small flame danced before them to guide their way.

Idris offered a slight bow. "As you wish."

Loren took a small step down the passage. "Could have fought me a little harder on that one."

"Would you like me to?"

Loren sighed and led them into the deep dark. "Let's just get this over with."

CHAPTER TWELVE

They walked for what felt like miles. What appeared to be a straightaway turned ever so slightly, and each bend offered nothing but more darkness ahead. Loren kept the pace steady but slow. Aram's breathing behind him sounded labored; Idris helped the king along the path with a paw at his side at all times.

The tunnel was an impossibility. There were structures beneath the cove, sewer lines, maintenance hatches, and the like, yet they never came across any of them. Even the tunnel itself, the physical structure of it, mystified the detective. No beams supported the roof. No debris kicked along the ground with their movements. Everything was smooth, as if sculpted by hand rather than constructed with equipment.

Loren's hand settled against the nearest wall. The lighter offered little in the way of details in the thick black. Where dirt should have welcomed him, obsidian rock glimmered along the surface in a solid wave.

"What is this?" he asked, more to himself than anyone else. Would Portents always confuse the hell out of him? What else had he missed over the years in his ignorance?

"The gateway to the tomb," Idris replied matter-of-factly. Nothing about their location disturbed the lion somehow.

"It's impossible, though," Loren said. "These walls. This isn't—"

"Detective," Aram said in his soft voice. "We are no longer in your city. We have crossed into the folds between worlds."

"But the subway tunnel? Soriya heard the construction, but these walls couldn't have been carved with any machinery. Not with how smooth they are."

Aram nodded. "They wouldn't use anything other than their own brute strength."

"You think this was done by hand?" Loren shook his head. He continued to the next bend in the tunnel, the way back completely lost to view. "That's absurd."

Rounding the curve in the tunnel, Loren's light fell upon figures in the dark. Six shadows stepped forward. The one in the lead grumbled loudly.

"No," he said. "That's craftsmanship."

"Holy!" Loren jumped back at their arrival. He nudged Aram in his haste, which forced Idris to take hold of the king to steady him. The dim light from Loren's Zippo flickered before it settled once more on the newcomers.

Thick beards covered in muck and sweat filled their faces. Scratches ran along their exposed skin. Calloused hands held tight to tools—axes and shovels. They stood no taller than Loren's waist. Stubby legs carried them closer.

"Are you…"

Idris growled under his breath. "Dwarves."

The lead dwarf swatted at Loren's lighter, but missed. "Get that light out of my face, surface dweller," he snarled in a deep voice.

At his left, one of his brethren—this one thinner with bulbous eyes of green—leaned in close. "They prefer humans, I think, Grimdul."

The leader spat as he spoke. "I'll call them what I like, Scud."

Loren stared madly at the group. Even though they stood directly before him, something in the back of his brain struggled to acknowledge the reality of his situation. His night had taken him far from the Annex's cold cases.

Distracted, Loren failed to notice one dwarf shift next to him. With a grin on his face, he blew at the lighter, knocking out the flame with a giggle.

Loren reeled his hand back and flicked the small flame back into place.

Aram cleared his throat. "Is the work complete, Master Dwarf?"

"Straight to business." Grimdul clasped his hands together with excitement. "Can tell who wears the crown around here."

Again, the giggling dwarf blew out the lighter. Loren nudged him away, flicking the Zippo on once more.

"Stop that," he snapped.

"No," replied the chuckling dwarf.

"Grimdul?" Aram called calmly, though Loren could tell the king's patience waned in the sharpness of his eyes.

"Aye, it's done." Grimdul inched forward, an accusing finger pointed at them. "Or will be when our deal is complete. Have you brought our payment?"

Idris stepped forward and slapped away the dwarf's finger. "Greedy bottom feeders. I should take your head for speaking to my lord in such a manner."

Grimdul grinned at his brethren. They all shared a laugh. "Do so and no tomb, hairbag."

Loren washed the lighter over the group, trying to soak in every detail about them.

Grimdul backed away into the dark. "Last warning on the light, boy."

Loren fought a smile. The dwarves appeared to be little more than children themselves, despite their beards. "Who are you calling *boy*?"

Snarls through clenched jaws responded to Loren's tone. The group gripped their tools tighter and raised them from their sides.

Aram stepped ahead of Loren. As he passed, he lowered the light so it was only a dim circle near the wall. From within the king's cloak, Aram retrieved the jingling satchel. He held it before him.

"Your payment, Grimdul," Aram said. "Take it with my appreciation."

The giggling dwarf snatched the bag from the king's hand. Grimdul did the same to his companion, letting the weight of the satchel settle against his palm, as if he could figure out the payment through the bag's burlap.

He bounced the bag along his palm, then caught it by the string. "I think we'll just take it."

Laughter erupted through the group. They pushed past Loren and Idris, mindful of the king—a clear sign of the small amount of respect they had to offer—and started back toward the subway tunnel. The clinking of gold coins passed between them, though Grimdul was quick to snatch any loose ones back from his brethren.

Loren listened to them for a long moment, then shook his head. "Hey," he called into the dark. "What about the tomb? How much farther is it?"

Grimdul stopped. "Can't you tell?"

He snapped his fingers.

Light filled the tunnel behind the trio. Loren slowly turned to see a cavern open at the end of the straightaway. Beyond the light stood a structure in white—the tomb.

When he looked to thank the dwarves, they were gone.

Aram's hand fell on Loren's shoulder. "They do love their work. Come. We're almost there."

CHAPTER THIRTEEN

The eggs were growing. Soriya felt them shifting around her insides, through the open wound on her side. The green ooze congealed. It took shape and squirmed with her every movement.

"Come on," she muttered along the sidewalk in front of Aram's home. "It can't be that bad. Just look. You can do it. Just…"

Pustules ran along the ridge of the cut. Below the surface were the eggs. They rapidly multiplied by pulling in the foreign material and taking shape. Soriya tried to run away from the sight, but it was part of her now. There was no enemy to fight. The battle was one of survival, and she was losing.

"Oh. Oh, God."

Short, frantic breaths escaped her lungs. She closed her eyes to calm her nerves. Every soothing technique failed.

"The wound…" It wasn't bad. An inch to the left and Ur would have killed her. Some stitches could close the gap and keep her upright for a nice, long life. "But the eggs…"

Soriya had never been one to give in to fear. For her entire life—what she recalled, at least—she'd fought against every enemy in her path. She had stood against myths of old and monsters straight out of nightmares. None had given her pause. Soriya had fought them and won, with or without help, because that was who she was. She was the Greystone, and no one would keep her from protecting her city.

Now, though, only fear remained. Panic raced through her veins faster than her blood could carry it. She couldn't catch her breath, couldn't see straight or think clearly. There was only the sound of the shifting eggs in her gut and the thought of them spilling forth.

Her end played behind her eyes. She saw her body split apart at the birth of Ur's children, then served as their first meal.

Soriya shook her head and forced a false grin. "Who knew motherhood could be so terrifying?"

Pain shot through her abdomen. Soriya clutched tight to the wound; the remnants of the ooze coated her fingers. Screaming, she curled up close to Aram's stoop, discomforted by the light of the moon for allowing her a better view of her impending death.

The eggs were now visible. The shells started to harden. Time slipped away quicker and quicker, her own body the best incubator for evil she had ever seen.

Soriya drew in a deep breath and bit her lip hard. "Can't let it end like this. Won't let it."

The hand-woven pouch along her right hip swung along her belt as she rolled over. Reaching inside, Soriya removed the Greystone. There was only one choice left to her, though the consequences frightened her as much as doing nothing.

Warmth from the stone pulsed up her arm. She took that surge and sent it right back to the source. With every ounce of strength left, her thoughts focused on one goal: survival.

Flames flickered along her flesh. Heat from the rising fire seared her skin. Soriya jammed the stone against the wound and focused her efforts on the mounting infection. Boils overtook the pustules, which burst in agony at the intense heat drawn through the stone.

More screams filled the air. Pain, the likes of which she had never felt before, fueled her own. Ur's unborn children joined the chorus; their cries echoed in the night as flames engulfed the eggs. Their pleas for survival were lost over her own.

As they silenced, Soriya continued to concentrate on the task.

Her vision blurred; black dots filled the periphery. Unconsciousness threatened to take her and she bit harder on her lip, cutting through the skin to keep herself going.

She had to be sure, to know without a doubt the threat had been neutralized. If even one egg remained, it might finish her in her weakened state.

The last of the pustules burst. Fluid spilled onto the sidewalk and spread away from her body. Soriya caught sight of the embryos, cooked through and dead.

With her task complete, she poured what strength remained through the stone. Soriya focused on the cut itself. She pinched her skin together, and the heat did the rest, sealing the wound up by cooking her flesh.

The wound was a mangled mess. It was, however, no longer bleeding or breeding.

Soriya fought for breath as the stone dimmed. She tried to heal from the efforts undertaken, but there was nothing left for her to give to the Greystone.

Her hand caught the railing above and pulled. Slowly, she made it to her feet. The trail of her companions spread out before her, a long walk on an even longer night.

The thought of it made her cringe. Her side sent waves of anguish through her with each step. A quiet glance to her left brought the Ribbons of Kali to life. They shot around her abdomen, wrapping tight to secure the wound and everything left loose from her unorthodox surgery. The wound continued to burn, but it held together until the pain diminished slightly.

Soriya took another step, followed by another. "I need to move it," she said to herself. "He needs me. Loren needs me."

CHAPTER FOURTEEN

The tunnel opened up to a chamber. The ceiling shot up out of reach over twenty feet into the air. Every surface was polished; the rock face held no imperfections. Standing tall and in bright white marble were three structures.

Four wide steps led to twin doors of bronze on the building to the rear of the cavern. The doors stood open and inviting. Statues of kings wielding swords and battling demons were carved into the tomb's surface.

The other two structures were pillars shaped like obelisks. Their peaks glowed with the arrival of Loren and his companions. Pulsing light welcomed them to the chamber, which illuminated the entire place.

"You have got to be kidding me," Loren whispered as he stepped into the cavern. "This is… this is incredible."

How had something so magnificent been achieved? More than that, how could it remain connected to a place like Portents? What did it mean for his city and for the work he'd attempted to accomplish since joining the police department—since joining Soriya in her fight against the monsters and insanity that seemed to crop up nightly?

Terrible darkness followed him, things his nightmares would have nightmares about if Loren ever had the opportunity to contemplate his life. Yet, here he stood among the wonders of the world. Places of true beauty remained possible, undisturbed and brilliant against the growing shadows.

Loren pointed ahead. "All we do is walk you past those pillars and—"

The light of the pillars shook; the deep thrumming silenced and darkness flickered in the chamber. A horrible hum, like breath being exhaled by the earth itself, shot from the tunnel. Loren spun around and it washed over him in a wave, forcing his eyes to close for a moment.

When he opened them, Aram was falling.

"Aram?" Loren called. The king's legs had merely let go of his weight, and he dropped to the cavern floor. "Aram!"

Idris slid to the king's side, panic in his golden gaze. "My king…"

Aram smiled. Tears dotted his eyes. The light left him and the pillars dimmed further. They offered little more than a vague glimpse of their surroundings.

He reached up to his guardian. "I am your king no longer, I'm afraid."

"You can't," Idris pleaded. "Not when you're so close."

Aram struggled to catch his breath. His chest rose and fell rapidly. "The darkness was stronger than I prepared for," he said in a hushed voice. "The fault is mine, not yours. I'm sorry."

"I can carry you."

Aram shook his head. "It won't work. The sacrifice is mine, and mine alone, to make. The choice is part of the gift to the world." Tears poured loose. "Idris, my loyal guardian, I have a much greater burden for you now."

His hand shook; fingers threatened to curl up and never spread again. Aram reached within his cloak. The skandola returned with him and he held it out before him.

Idris stared at the talisman. The power contained within it helped keep the evil of Ur locked away for millennia. It had always been carried by royalty, by the great line of kings—as far as Loren knew. Idris let the token settle along his paw, feeling the weight of the task passed to him.

"Shoulder it well." Aram beamed at his guardian. "Our time together… it was a gift I will always cherish."

"As will I," Idris replied through choked back tears.

Aram squeezed Idris' paw shut over the skandola. Gratitude spread across his face in the form of a sad smile—happy to have the lion at his side, yet clearly regretful over passing along his burden.

With a soft exhale, the king closed his eyes. His chest failed to rise. His hand slipped from Idris and fell to his side, where it rested on the cavern floor.

Loren stood in shock. The cavern continued to illuminate through the pillars before the tomb, but with each passing second, the steady hum grew more and more inconsistent. The pulsing slowed, and the light faded.

Every corner of the enormous space fell into shadow. The ceiling vanished behind a wall of darkness. Even the tomb did not seem to be immune, the marble flecked with obsidian.

Idris growled, the sound a mournful wail for the dead. The king was gone, and with it all chance of holding back Ur's evil.

"What do we do now?" Loren asked.

The lion struggled to find a response. Without the king, there was no sacrifice to make and no chance to end the nightmare that had claimed their night.

Soundless in their approach, shadows flitted out of the passage. The soft exhale from before became a rush of wind that battered Loren and Idris. They slowly turned. The darkness was more than the dimming of the pillars.

The shadows opened up, and a figure emerged into the cavern. Ur had arrived.

"What do you do now?" the demon said maliciously. "You join him."

CHAPTER FIFTEEN

"Like hell, we will." Loren lifted his Glock from the holster and opened fire. Four shots boomed through the cavern. All were dead on target, aimed with murderous intent at the nightmare hunting them. Each one, however, passed through the shadows that made up the snake demon's body as if he was nothing but a wisp of air. They struck the wall behind Ur.

Loren groaned. He stared at his sidearm in disbelief. "Damn. I was really hoping that would work. Why does that never work?"

From the tunnel, the sound of chomping jaws carried into the cavern. Behind them came Ur's children. They took up position around their progenitor, their numbers lessened over the course of the night, but still more than a dozen.

Loren felt an ache rise from his chest. Their presence meant more than the end of their head start to the cavern. It meant Soriya had failed to stop the hatchlings and their master.

It meant Soriya...

Loren swiped at swollen eyes, tearful over the death of the king and now again at the potential loss of a woman he cared for more than he'd ever been able to understand. There was no time for grief or sadness. Loren now stood as the last line of defense.

Idris recognized their position as well. Mournful eyes caught Loren's. Silent nods passed between them as they accepted their role. They stepped away from the king to block the tomb from Ur.

The demon floated forward. His body still hovered above the

ground like a black cloud. His scaly fingers spread wide and his dark gaze flitted between the two guardians with widening arrogance.

"This is what the light has to offer as protection?" Ur asked. The shadows spread behind him, covering the exterior walls. They slowly seeped closer and closer along the interior. The dim light of the pillars, struggling to stay illuminated, kept them at bay. It was only a matter of time, though, before they failed, and Ur was happy to share the news with Loren and Idris. "A grief-stricken non-believer and an indoctrinated kitty-cat? Pathetic."

Idris snarled. He pounded the ground with his paws, ready to leap into battle. Loren held out his hand. He shook his head and begged for patience.

"I give you this one chance," Ur continued, his voice as slithery as his every movement. "Give me the skandola. The talisman for your lives. Think about it. There is no surviving my children. Not as you are. Take my offer and live."

Silence followed Ur's bargain, and the burden of their task grew with each stolen breath gained by the reprieve. Idris shook violently. Holding back was not his way, not in the face of the threat before them and not with the task forced upon him with Aram's death.

Loren, though, didn't know the best approach. He fought for time to figure out what to do and how to do it. He held up his hand to Ur, a look of concern as he shifted closer to his companion.

Idris snarled at the delay. Sharp nails caused small pinpricks into his palms to stem his bloodlust.

Loren pulled him close. "Idris?"

"The darkness lies," the lion replied simply. "That is all it knows how to do."

"I figured as much," Loren said with a sigh. He turned his back to Ur. Checking his Glock, Loren removed the spent clip for one of the spares he'd secured in his pocket before he'd left the Annex. He jammed it into place hard, then chambered the next round with a loud click.

"Any thoughts about how we do this?"

"We stop the darkness," Idris said. "Any way we have to.

That is all that matters now."

Loren nodded. He looked to the fallen king and then back to the talisman held tight by Idris. "He was right about the burden."

Idris stood taller. "It is one I carry proudly. But this is my task, Detective. It doesn't have to be yours."

Loren shook his head. "Yeah, pretty sure I feel the same, buddy. You ready for this?"

A roar erupted from the lion and he spun to meet his enemy. "Thank you," he muttered to Loren.

"Thank me if we live through this," Loren said, not liking their chances.

Idris held up the skandola. The talisman reflected what remained of the light as proudly as the beast carrying it. "If you want the skandola, Ur, come and get it."

Ur raised his hands to his sides. The shadows lifted him higher from the ground. From beneath his dark cloak, the hatchlings shot forward. "Children?" He pointed ahead. "Feeding time."

CHAPTER SIXTEEN

Idris launched at the hatchlings. They attacked with reckless abandon; their hunger made them desperate for their next meal, no matter the enemy against them. The lion snatched the first in mid-air, then slammed the snake into the ground. Its skull cracked beneath the massive paw of the guardian and died instantly.

Tucking the skandola beneath his armaments freed Idris' other hand for the fight. He swung wide and battered the leaping children of Ur. They flew back into the shadows, but no pain slowed them. The monsters were on their feet an instant later; they snapped their over-sized jaws in the air and raced for their victims.

Loren wished he had Idris' bulk to throw around. All the detective offered the fight was his gun. He fired at the rampaging hatchlings, which caused them to scatter around the fringes of the cavern. He clipped one in the back and it fell. Frantically spinning, the wounded creature struggled to reach the open wound without success. A second shot finished the snake off and ended its suffering.

Two more fell before the opening volley from Loren's Glock. Even with four down in a matter of seconds, the numbers remained against them.

Not only that, their breathing room slowly collapsed around them. It was barely noticeable at first, but when Loren rushed away from an approaching hatchling and stepped out of the protective light offered by the tomb's twin pillars, the shadows shot out—an ever-encroaching wall—and forced him back into the room's center.

The hatchling snapped at his ankle. Loren kicked at the beast, his sneaker little more than an annoyance. Tired of the foreplay, the snake leaped at Loren. The detective ducked, and the snake soared into the shadows. Loren staggered toward Idris, his gun ready for the snake's return.

"There are too many," Idris said.

"I'm aware," the detective intoned. A clicking sound rose from his weapon. Loren ejected the spent clip and inserted another in a fluid motion that took less than a second. "I'm running out of ammunition. Ideas?"

"None," Idris replied. A hatchling chomped down on his left arm. Blood poured from the exposed fangs of the snake. Idris reached over and ripped the beast from his arm. Holding him up, the lion snatched the snake's head between his paws and squeezed.

There was a loud pop; the guts of the monster spilled down the lion's front. Idris dropped his assailant and kicked the carcass aside. More approached, ready to replace their fallen brother.

Idris glanced at Loren. "I am sorry, Detective."

"Don't be," Loren said. His shot missed an approaching snake by inches. "And make it Greg."

The lion grinned. Ignoring the pain along his left arm, he shot up and his roar filled the cavern. "For King Aram and the light!"

The hatchlings surrounded the pair. Their snapping jaws offered a chorus of hate and their black eyes wanted nothing more than to consume everything in their path. None made their move, though, and when Loren peered up from the battle. Ur hovered over them all. His hand was raised, willing the children to stop with the silent motion.

"You fight for a dead man," Ur thundered from the dark. It echoed through every shadow in the cavern, repeating and rebounding through their ears. "Your king was nothing but a fool. Now, nothing but a memory."

Ur snapped his fingers. At his command, the hatchlings departed their prey and set upon the dead body of Aram like a shoal of piranhas. From head to toe, the king disappeared as they feasted. The children of Ur devoured his flesh, his bones, even the cloak he wore. All that remained were the tokens of his title—the jewels of the king… and his crown.

"No!" Idris cried. He rushed to where his lord had fallen. Swatting aside the monsters, who licked their lipless faces and picked the meat from between their jagged fangs, Idris cleared the way to Aram only to find nothing but the tarnished rings and adornments in a small heap.

He fell to his knees before the king's belongings. "He's truly gone now. How? How do I go on?"

Loren rushed to his side. He kept his gun leveled at the children, only to find them in a holding pattern. Ur, once again, kept them at bay without a single word spoken.

The detective's hand fell on the lion's shoulder and squeezed. "You have the talisman, Idris. There has to be something we can do. Think."

Idris shucked off Loren's hand, lost to his grief.

Ur grinned maliciously overhead. He clearly knew no options remained for them. The shadows grew like a wild forest; they threatened to overtake the entire cavern. Time was up and wasn't coming back, not without someone to intervene, not without someone standing up and taking the fight to the rising dark.

Loren peered around the room. He was the last option. No one else was left to carry the burden. Pushing away from Idris, Loren shuffled toward the tomb. He opened fire and took out two of the hatchlings before they could react.

With their deaths, the others hissed madly. They raged, jaws gnashing. The remains of their previous meal flew free, taunting Loren and the sanctity of the tomb. They raced for their next repast.

Loren shouted over the roar of the enemy and the firing of his gun. "You were with him for your entire life, Idris! In his service. At his side. Listening. Learning. He chose you. It had to be for a reason!"

At Loren's words, the lion woke to the room. Paws grazing his lord's final possessions with care dug through the pile—

suddenly aware of their situation and more.

Idris spun around with wide eyes. "I know what I have to do."

"Then do it already!" Loren said. The walls continued to close in, giving him little in the way of escape.

"I need time," Idris called from the other side of the chamber.

"You have none," Ur announced.

Idris paused on the rising darkness.

Loren shook him from his doubts. "Idris. You can do this."

"I have to," the lion confirmed. "Greg…"

"Do what you have to." Loren kicked at the surrounding beasts. "I'll give you as much time as I can. Somehow."

He fired at the snake by his toes. It leaped back before the bullet smashed into the ground. Loren lifted the Glock once more, only to hear the loud click of the empty clip. He was out of bullets and out of options.

From all around him, heat billowed. Flames erupted in a ring. Three hatchlings caught in the fire cooked. Their screams resounded in the cavern. The rest retreated.

Loren looked up toward the cavern's entrance. Soriya stood in the opening, the Greystone before her.

"How about a helping hand?"

CHAPTER SEVENTEEN

Soriya's body screamed for relief. Her journey had been pure torture; her wound had begged for attention, and she'd offered none. All that had mattered was reaching Loren in time—to make sure he'd survived and their task had been completed.

Her arrival wasn't a total success in that regard. Aram was nowhere to be found, though Soriya picked up a clue or ten from the sorrowful lion kneeling over the king's jewels.

The light continued to dim, despite her presence. The sudden influx of heat had wiped out a vast swath of hatchlings. Their cries echoed throughout the chamber as they died.

There was still work to be done, and injury or no injury, Soriya took flight—leaping at Ur with the Greystone before her. The demon snake shimmered in the air before he melded into nothing more than shadow. It was exactly as she had planned.

Soriya tucked the stone to her hip, dove through the shadows, and landed at Loren's side. Rolling from the impact, she flipped up to her feet to face the shocked detective with a smirk.

Loren looked her over, then shook his head. "We need to work on your timing."

Soriya spun around. She shot out her foot and caught a hatchling in the head. It tumbled away, slamming into three more like bowling pins before all four crashed to the ground.

"My timing was pretty perfect." Soriya brushed the hair clear from her face. "You did know I was coming, right?"

"Of course," Loren replied, though his wayward gaze told a different story.

"You didn't."

"I did," he snapped back defensively. His shoulders shrugged slightly. "I mean, I hoped."

She nodded. "I'll take it."

Loren pointed at the recovered children of Ur. "How about you take them instead?" He lifted his gun. "This thing is little more than a paperweight at this point."

Soriya took the hint and cut Loren off from the fight. With the Greystone back in her hand, the snakes hissed their discontent. Soriya chuckled. Everything hurt. Her entire body was nothing more than a bruise, ripped open, cut through, and stapled back together on repeat, thanks to her desperation.

However, with Loren at her back, Soriya felt rejuvenated in the best way possible. Something about the man, something about the way he trusted her with a world he knew nothing about, raised her spirits.

Whenever she fell, Loren lifted her up, and she swore to do the same no matter what came between them. There was balance in their relationship—a pure symmetry. She needed his strength, and he delivered, as he always had. She hoped he always would.

The stone lit, powered by her renewed strength. Fire danced around them like a barrier and forced the hatchlings to hesitate. They gazed at their lord and master, begging for a reprieve.

Ur ushered them forward with only a gesture.

When they leaped at Soriya, she twisted the stone around.

The flames faded immediately and a powerful breeze caught the tiny monsters in mid-air. They hung in the open for a long second—staring at each other with open jaws and confused eyes—then the wind slammed them back. They shot through the shadows and hit the cavern wall.

Buying them a few seconds took its toll, however. Her will drained quickly from the effort.

Looking back, Soriya hoped for a plan from Loren. What she found was her friend's worried gaze on the still grieving lion.

"Idris?" Loren asked. "Maybe speed things up."

The guardian growled. The pressure was definitely unwanted. His prayers slipped from his lips, quiet for him, but the words echoed in the confines of the cavern.

"You named me for a reason," Idris said to the dead king, now only a memory. "You gifted me so much, yet I must ask for one more."

"What is he doing?"

Before Loren could answer Soriya's question, shards of shadow snapped in their direction. Little spikes of Ur's shroud came to life and sought to impale the pair of protectors.

Loren shoved Soriya to the right, just missing a pair of shadowy daggers. Soriya snatched Loren's wrist to pull him clear with her as another wave blanketed over them.

The pair fell hard to the ground. They rolled over each other until they were clear of the attack.

Loren's eyes widened, and he fell off her. Dusting himself off, he staggered to his feet.

Soriya bounded up. "Well? Any idea what Idris is up to?"

"How should I know?" Loren said. "Idris!"

The lion took a deep breath. Shadows surrounded him, closing in fast. As they did, the guardian rose from the ashes of his king. In his hands, Idris held tight to a single item found among what remained of Aram.

"There will always be a king."

"Idris?" Loren asked in confusion. "What are you doing?"

"What I must."

Ur's eyes blazed in black. His shadows reached for the lion. "It can't be."

Idris lifted Aram's fallen crown. The moment it fell upon his head, Idris' entire body lit up like a star. Behind him, the pillars blazed anew.

The lion growled with power. "I am the last of the great kings of this world—the final light against the darkness."

CHAPTER EIGHTEEN

"Depart this realm, Ur," Idris announced. He glowed as bright as a small sun within the confines of the cavernous tomb. Loren squinted to view the lion shining beneath Aram's crown. Within his paw, he lifted the skandola. The talisman taunted Ur with its very presence.

Something about the lion had changed in the simple act of placing the crown on his head. Something had triggered a spark within the mythic guardian, a growth in spirit and stature. Idris appeared regal, a lord among lions and men alike.

He held the talisman higher. "Leave, Ur, before it is too late."

"You do not frighten me, false king," Ur spat. His forked tongue hung out of his mouth, whipping wildly at his enemy in anger. He spread his arms before him, unafraid. "My darkness continues to thrive and your light already falters."

Ur was right. Even with the sudden blaze at Idris' ascension to the metaphorical throne of the world, the light had already begun to fade. The lion slowly came back into view, though his presence had changed somehow by taking on the crown. He appeared older, with flecks of gray in his mane and around the gold of his eyes.

"Idris," Loren called with a million questions on his lips. Soriya, unfortunately, beat him to it.

"The king gave him the skandola?" she asked, amazement on her face.

"Yeah," Loren said. "Before he died." Flicking his finger, Loren showed the spot where Aram fell, only to find it vacant.

"Well, he was there before he was eaten, anyway. I don't want to see that again, by the way. It was really gross."

Soriya grinned at him. She somehow always enjoyed his discomfort with their work together. "Aram transferred more than the talisman, then," she explained. "Idris was his guardian—a king's guardian. The only way he would be chosen for the role is if he carried royal blood of his own. From the Nemeans."

"Nemeans?" Loren shot back. He had a sudden flashback to high school history class. It had involved way too much hair down the back of his neck and an awkward mustache, but some learning had happened every once in a while, too. "Like the lion that wrestled Hercules?"

Soriya's mouth sat agape in stunned silence.

Loren rolled his eyes at the unspoken insult. "Hey, I know some stuff."

She patted his back with pride. It wasn't exactly the emotion Loren felt with the gesture, but he let it slide. Soriya beamed at the crowned lion. "A king of all lion-kind. Imagine that."

"Yeah," Loren said, joining her in their approval of their newfound friend.

"Fall back, Ur," Idris decreed, the snarl clear on his lips. "This is your last warning."

Ur seethed. Fists clenched, he slipped from the shadows and shot them out in a rage. "I will strip the flesh from your bones myself!"

Slices of darkness slammed into the ground with the force of explosions. They cracked the cavern's once immaculate surface, forcing the trio of guardians to scatter for cover. Loren stuck close to Soriya, cut off from Idris in the melee.

"Ur seems to be taking the news well," Loren muttered.

The shadows sharpened on all sides. They cut through the air, no longer satisfied watching from the corners of the vast room.

Soriya snatched Loren by the collar and pulled him down as a wave washed over them. The shadows rushed by, a few strands of hair cut a little shorter as they passed.

"Whoa!" he exclaimed.

Soriya pushed him back, shielding his body despite her own

apparent injuries. "Get to safety, Loren. Idris and I can handle Ur."

"It is my task, stone bearer," Idris announced. "I have to—"

So concerned for their safety, the lion missed the massing shadows behind him. Ur was there in a flash. He slipped from the darkness like he was shedding his skin. From out of the shadows, his razor-sharp claws shot forward and silenced the newly crowned king.

"What?" Ur hissed into the lion's ear with glee. "What must you do? Because it looks like the only thing you will ever do… is die."

The blow sliced through Idris' midsection—armor and all—as if he was nothing but meat. Ur lifted the impaled lion up from the earth, hovering higher than ever. Idris cried out. Blood filled his mouth and dripped from his lips.

"Idris!" Loren screamed. Soriya held him back, both only able to watch the awful display unfold.

"A false king, through and through," the darkness bellowed.

The claws retracted. Idris fell to the ground and landed on his knees. His hands clutched tight to the wound, unable to stem the tide of dark crimson escaping between his mighty fingers.

The skandola fell from his grasp. In his agony, the token slipped free and bounded away to the cavern's open expanse.

One of the remaining hatchlings picked it up. It carried the talisman carefully to the shadows drifting before him. Ur was suddenly there, and he took the ancient icon in hand.

"Finally," Ur said in triumph. "The skandola is mine. And with it, this world."

CHAPTER NINETEEN

"No!" Loren pushed through the growing shadows of the cavern.

"Loren," Soriya called, too late to stop him. "Don't!"

Loren fell into the darkness that spread from Ur's being. When he came out, he was at Idris' side, sliding along the earth with hands reaching to assist.

"Idris," he said in a quiet voice. Soriya wanted to follow but held back, barring the remaining hatchlings from taking advantage of the situation. Loren continued to kneel at the lion's side, hands over the gaping wound and blood-stained paws of their friend. "What can I do? How can I—"

Idris choked on his own blood. He struggled to clear his throat, rolling to his side slightly, though the movement obviously pained him. Deep breaths and closed eyes refocused him.

"The talisman," the lion said, pointing ahead. "It grounds him."

Both turned at the revelation. Neither had noticed the shift, but Idris had picked up on it immediately. The second the skandola was in the grip of Ur, the demon of the underworld stopped hovering over them. His feet rested on the ground. In fact, for the first time since their meeting, they could see every inch of Ur. Head to toe, his entire body was now exposed. His physical form was trapped in the world, thanks to his possession of the skandola.

Loren shot her a look. "Soriya?"

She nodded. "I see it."

Ur continued to revel in his dominance. He held the skandola up like a trophy—triumphant and unafraid. The rest of them realized something completely different in his so-called victory. They saw a chance when there had been none before. They saw hope and held it even tighter than the demon did to the sacred talisman.

Soriya bent at the knees. Her hands balled up into fists, and her eyes locked on her target. "You ready?"

Loren stood from Idris' side. "Kick his ass already."

"Gladly."

Soriya raced at Ur with a smirk on her face. She cocked her right fist back, then shot forward. The blow connected against the snake's cheek and he staggered back two steps.

"Y—You—" Ur stammered. "You dare?"

Shadow spears shot from his cloak. They cratered around Soriya. She dove through them, spinning like a pinwheel to get out of the firing line. Once clear, she looped around for another pass at Ur. She refused to be pushed back, to be sent away, for a single second. It didn't matter how badly her body screamed or how much she felt her wound reopening beneath the mystical Ribbons of Kali. This was their one chance.

Ur shook his head, the skandola firmly in hand. "There is no winning here, child."

Finally aware of his sudden vulnerability, Ur stepped behind the wall of his own darkness. His children rushed forward in his defense, snapping and clawing at the air.

Soriya batted them away, unafraid and unwilling to postpone the true fight ahead. The hatchlings bellowed in pain as they were beaten back. They fell to the ground in silence at their failure.

Her path cleared, Soriya ripped into the shadows. She pulled back the curtain Ur wrapped himself in and delivered another blow to the face. The demon's shadows pierced her flesh; they dug into her arms and legs, but she continued to carry on until she was directly before Ur.

"You fight without purpose," Ur sneered. "With the skandola, this world is mine. I control everything."

"What about without it?" Soriya raised the Greystone before her.

"What are you—"

The rune showered the surface of the stone with light and surged outward. White spread in a wave; her will caused the intense illumination to scream throughout the chamber.

The shadows scurried away before they were enveloped in her blast. Ur tried to defend himself. His hands covered the terror spread across his face. As he did, the skandola fell to the ground.

"Loren!" Soriya cried as she pressed the stone further. Each step forced Ur back until the talisman was in the open on the cavern floor.

"Got it," Loren said. Fingers wrapped carefully around the sacred object.

"No," Ur grimaced, unable to see in the center of the light storm. His shadows were gone, his body little more than a wisp of black against the brilliance of the Greystone's energy.

"Hurry," Soriya said, the word barely a whisper. Her strength ebbed from the strain. "Hurry, Loren. He's reforming."

The light flickered as the rune faded from view. Soriya staggered a step. The world spun wildly in front of her. She fell to her knees as her arms spread to her sides, limp and broken.

"And I'm all out of tricks."

CHAPTER TWENTY

Loren held the skandola. For such a prized possession, it appeared to be little more than an over-sized bus token. There was some weight to it, thanks to the gold base and the embossed images along the surface, but there was nothing extraordinary about the piece in his hands.

To the rest of the room, however, the skandola controlled the fate of the world. Light versus dark. Good versus evil. They were constant battles, but they were built on choice. The talisman took that away somehow—making their roles in the drama little more than bit players instead of instruments of free will.

Loren chalked his opinion up to his own ignorance, something Soriya had always been able to point out. But she was down. Her body had given way from the effort displayed by the Greystone. With her no longer able to keep Ur at bay, it was up to Loren to save the day.

He rushed back to Idris. The bleeding lion pulled at the earth beneath his paws. Inch by inch, he crawled along the ground to reach the pillars. Loren crouched at his side. With every ounce of strength he had, Loren lifted the great guardian.

"On your feet, your majesty."

Idris groaned in pain. With his other hand, he continued to cover his gaping wound. Idris could barely keep his eyes open. His tongue lolled out of the side of his mouth as if begging for a drink.

"Barnabas…" he muttered, lost in the memory of his fallen brother-in-arms. "He said there would be nights like this."

Loren helped the lion forward. "He was a wise friend."

"It seems I have more than one now," Idris said. He padded along, but at the third step, tumbled.

Loren caught him, straining against the lion's weight. "Come on now. Work with me a little."

"What does it look like I'm doing?"

"Like you're giving up," Loren said. "I know you better than that."

Idris shook his head. Spatters of blood dripped down his mane. "My fight is over."

"No, it isn't," Loren snapped. "Not by a long shot."

Idris pulled away, but Loren held firm. He locked the lion down and dragged him ahead.

"Listen to me now," the detective said in a firm tone. "Who else will fight for this world, Idris? Who else can? This is your task. Aram gave his life. What are you willing to give?"

The lion choked back the blood filling his lungs and roared. He stood tall to push ahead. This time when he stumbled, Loren was there as a support instead of carrying the guardian's full weight.

"That's it," Loren said. "I'm right here with you." He looked back for a moment. "Soriya?"

Her eyes struggled to focus on him. She waved, then collapsed on her side.

The delay she'd granted them quickly ran out. From all around the cavern, the shadows returned. They overtook the light from the pillars. The entire room dropped into darkness. Rising from the cavern entrance, they created a wall of shadow and rushed toward the fleeing pair.

Ur's voice bellowed through them all; his taunting tone surrounded Loren. "I won't let you stop me now! My time has arrived. This world craves the darkness. It was built for my kind."

Idris shook his head. Ur's beliefs served as nothing more than motivation for him to keep going.

"You're wrong," he said. Idris turned to Loren, golden gaze wide and alive. "There is still light in this realm. It will always be here for those willing to see it."

Loren took in every word. They echoed through his mind and settled deep in his heart. He knew he would carry them with him for the rest of his life.

Their steps quickened in tune with the rushing shadows at their backs. The pillars loomed over them, flickering and fading.

"Take this." Loren passed along the skandola.

Idris took it in hand.

"Almost there." Loren pressed another step forward, and they were before the twin pillars. White marble stood on either side. "The pillars, Idris. We can—"

"Not we," Idris interrupted. He held out his arm. "You have to let me go, Greg."

Loren hesitated.

Idris winked at him. "My burden, remember?"

Loren backed away from the towering lion. His steps carried him from the pillars toward the shadows.

Idris staggered forward with the skandola before him and the crown atop his head.

The shadows roared in anger. "No! I refuse to surrender this world. I will have the skandola!"

Loren lost sight of the world as darkness enveloped all. The shadows ate away at the marble of the pillars. They picked away every fleck of luminescence, bounding in anger at the tomb and the lion at the heart of it all.

"The skandola is mine!"

For an instant, everything went black. Loren dreamed the world was lost, that their task failed and everything fell to the darkness. It was a chilling moment and evidence of the precarious nature of their existence—always at risk, yet always worth fighting for in the end.

Then the light returned. Slowly, at first, and from one step beyond the pillars, the light grew from a single, innocuous token before it spread everywhere.

Idris stood at the center with the skandola held high. "Not in this lifetime. Goodbye, Ur."

The darkness screamed as light flooded the cavern and spread out through the tunnel to the world beyond. Ur's cries faded, just as he and his children did, until only the light remained.

CHAPTER TWENTY-ONE

Soriya fought her way to her feet. The world continued to spin, and she closed her eyes tight to combat the vertigo threatening to send her back to the ground. Deep breaths centered her. Slowly, she opened her eyes again. Light beamed from the tomb's pillars.

Loren stood before them. He spun around to scan for the enemy that had nearly destroyed them. Beyond the pillars was Idris. He glowed like a star. His wounds were no longer bleeding. The skandola rested against his palm.

"You did it," Loren said to Idris. "You won."

"Almost," the lion replied. Sadness filled his deep, golden eyes. "My task isn't quite complete, Greg."

Loren's brow furrowed. He glanced back at Soriya, who approached as quickly as her body would allow. A hand rested over the Ribbons of Kali and she felt the heat rush through her body. When Loren twisted toward Idris again, he asked, "What are you talking about?"

Loren stepped forward. The ends of his sneakers ran along the pillar's edge. Soriya rushed ahead and caught him before he could move another inch.

"Loren, stop."

The startled and confused detective reached out. His hand sought the open air between the pillars, but found an invisible barrier in place. It crackled beneath his fingertips. Minor shocks ran up his skin; a chill pulsed through his body. It increased the more he pressed against the barrier.

Soriya joined him. Her fingers grazed the invisible wall. She saw it in the tired eyes of the lion and in the glow emanating from his body. There were places even she couldn't go in the world. Some tasks were meant for others.

"Idris." Loren banged his hand against the barrier. "Knock it off. We can get you fixed up."

Idris shook his head. His paw showed the bloodless wound in his gut. The hole through his abdomen remained—the six-inch gap went all the way through. There was no fixing that, no healing from an injury so egregious.

"I'm already gone," the lion confirmed. "This is how it has to be."

"Why?"

Soriya's hand settled on Loren's shoulder and squeezed. "The king has to die to save us, Loren. The skandola takes his sacrifice, using that power—that light—to protect the world from evil."

"You said it before, my friend," Idris said with a bow of his head. "This is my task."

Loren slammed his open hands against the barrier. "Idris. There has to be something we can do. Don't feed me that line. This isn't a task. This is your death."

"One and the same," Idris answered. "You have your own task, Greg. Make it mean something. For yourself. For every-one."

"Idris, don't!"

The lion's paw reached out. He touched the barrier opposite Loren. Tears fell free from Loren's eyes and spilled to the ground at his feet.

"Farewell, my friend," the fallen king said, a sad smile on his face. With that, he turned for the open doors of the tomb. His steps were no longer labored, his pain gone like his mortality—shed away with all the weight that had come with his burden. Idris crossed the barrier of the doors and disappeared into the darkness within.

Loren's head rested along the barrier. He swiped at his eyes as his friend faded from the world.

"Farewell," he whispered.

The doors to the tomb closed. The light from the twin pillars gleamed brightly; they pulsed in a steady rhythm as waves washed out through the cavern and into the world. It was protection against Ur and creatures like him. No demons would be welcome for quite some time, thanks to Idris.

Loren turned his back to the tomb. He settled against the pillar and sank to the ground. Soriya joined him. Wrapping an arm around him, she pulled Loren close.

"We'll never see this place again, will we?" Loren asked.

"No," Soriya said. "The tunnel will seal behind us."

"Like it was never here," Loren muttered. He glanced at the closed tomb. "Like *he* was never here."

Soriya joined him, peering around the immense cavern as if for the first time. It was a wonder to behold, especially the etchings on the tomb. She could have sworn they had held kings of old, as they held back the darkness to safeguard the world. Looking now, however, they weren't faceless figures from an unknowable past, but the images of Aram and Idris. Both towered proudly over them. Each held the talisman and, from the center, they glowed.

Their presence made her smile.

"We'll know." She stood and held out her hands.

Loren took her hands. He stood beside his friend and partner. At the tunnel's entrance, Loren paused to look back.

"Loren," Soriya called. "We'll know."

He struggled with the thought. Pain filled his tired eyes. A nod escaped him, and he joined her for the trip back into the world.

"Yeah, we will," he said. "Always."

CHAPTER TWENTY-TWO

Silence dominated the long walk back. Thoughtful contemplation carried them out of the dwarf tunnel and through Portents to Venture Cove.

A cool wind soothed Loren's skin. He opened his coat to invite the breeze inside, hoping it might wipe away the heat and so much more from the evening's adventure.

He couldn't help but ponder everything that had happened. From the death of Barnabas and the rise of the hatchlings, to meeting Aram, Idris, and a pack of dwarves, there were new emotions with every circumstance, but all added up to what had been lost through their trials.

Idris' death hurt the most—their connection the deepest during their journey. Though their time together had been limited, they had been fast friends, and Loren already missed what potential there might have been in their friendship.

Despite the loss, the tightness in Loren's chest lifted the farther he traveled into the night. A sense of calm—of acceptance, almost—settled over him, and each breath ached a little less than the last. Idris' sacrifice pained him, but the great lion had died saving the world. He had fulfilled his lifelong task by seeing Aram's through. It was a hell of a way to go, and Loren envied the guardian for reaching the finish line with style and grace.

As they neared the Annex, Loren glanced at Soriya. She stuck close to his side, always within reach, just like she had been since the day they'd met. He never understood why she had chosen him—the mystery continued to elude him—but his gratitude for her presence grew with each encounter. Soriya had saved him, as she had dozens of times in the past. Despite all his failings, she continued to stand by him, and he was lucky to have her.

A smile sparked across his face. Of course, there was every possibility nothing like tonight would have happened to Loren in the first place had he never met Soriya. He would simply continue to work the cases on his desk, the insurmountable task as Idris had called it. Part of him dreamed of it, but another—a truer part, perhaps—knew he would miss the wonder of Soriya's world, even with the pain that came with it. Loren didn't think he could bear the trade-off.

Soriya, silent and stoic at his side, tried her best to hide her pain. The night had certainly taken a greater toll on her. She held tight to her side. The pink ribbon squeezed against her flesh, but through the thick strands Loren noticed the raw, burned flesh.

"You should get that looked at."

"It will be fine," Soriya replied. Catching his glare, she tossed him a dismissive wave. "I'll have Mentor fix me up. Promise."

The Annex loomed before them. Chips in the door hung loosely from the wood. The broken railing lay in a twisted heap on the side of the large stoop. Loren took to the first step, before Soriya called him back.

"The world would have fallen into darkness if not for Idris, Loren," she said. "If not for you."

"Me?" Loren exclaimed. "What good was I?"

"Plenty," she answered with a smirk. "Believe me. Believe Idris."

The lion had called him friend. Of all the things in the world, Loren found that to be the most difficult to believe, yet he held onto it with all his heart. The last king had been his friend, and had seen in him a kindred spirit, fighting against the dark— never retreating or surrendering, no matter the odds against them.

Loren nodded to Soriya. "Right."

"Need a hand in there?" she asked, a thumb at the cracked and splintered doors.

"Nay." Loren jammed his hands into his pockets and swayed on his heels. "It can't be that bad."

Soriya paused at the shadows dominating the block. "Be kind

to yourself, Loren," she said. "It may be your task, but it isn't yours alone."

Loren chuckled. "That your way of saying, *see you soon?*"

"I'm sure I will."

The detective stared up into the night. The stars gleamed brighter for him. "Next apocalypse, right? Soriya?"

When he shifted back to the sidewalk, she was gone. Loren left the stoop of the Annex, scanning right and left for signs of her, though he knew there wouldn't be any.

"I will never get used to that."

Loren took to the steps. He ignored the broken railing and cracked slabs of wood. All that mattered were the cases waiting to be closed and the lives waiting for answers.

The task was his. It always would be. The work would never be insurmountable, because he would never be alone in handling it.

Confidently, Loren whipped the doors to the Annex open, ready to face the challenges of his work and his life. What met him was the utter destruction of the bullpen area. Desks were little more than piles of sawdust on the floor. The thick tarps on top of the furniture throughout the room were all but gone, except for a few strands that hung limply against half-eaten chairs and tables. Lying on the ground was the coffee machine; liquid remnants spread in a pool beside the shattered pot.

The hatchlings' wrath was clear in every direction and followed his every step into the Annex. Loren rubbed at the back of his neck.

"This will be fun to explain."

Ignoring the devastation for the moment and praying the conversation would never come, Loren entered his temporary office and closed the door. The file remained open on his desk.

There was a murder to solve.

The work never ended, and Greg Loren wouldn't have it any other way.

ABOUT THE AUTHOR

Lou Paduano is the author of the Greystone series of urban fantasy adventures, which follow Detective Greg Loren and Soriya Greystone as they hunt myths, monsters, and legends in the city of Portents.

He is also the author of the conspiracy thriller series, The DSA, a serialized tale about a clandestine government agency trying to discover the true power behind humanity's future.

Lou lives with his wife and three daughters in Grand Island, NY. You can learn more about his books, including upcoming releases and free content by visiting his website at loupaduano.com.

THE GREYSTONE SAGA

AVAILABLE NOW

Follow the adventures of Soriya Greystone and Detective Greg Loren as they hunt dangerous myths and legends in the city of Portents.

BOOK ONE - SIGNS OF PORTENTS
BOOK TWO - TALES FROM PORTENTS
BOOK THREE - THE MEDUSA COIN
BOOK FOUR - PATHWAYS IN THE DARK
BOOK FIVE - A CIRCLE OF SHADOWS

GREYSTONE-IN-TRAINING

AVAILABLE NOW

For years, Soriya trained to become the Greystone.
Follow the trials that made her the protector
Portents needed to fend off the darkest of threats.

BOOK ONE - HAMMER AND ANVIL
BOOK TWO - THE GIFTS OF KALI
BOOK THREE - THE FINAL GAUNTLET

GREYSTONE CONTINUES IN:

The Kindly Killer stalks the streets of Portents…

Detective Greg Loren searches for a madman. The case is his final lifeline, the last vestige of hope holding him together after the death of his wife.

He can't do it alone.

Soriya Greystone knows this and offers him a partnership like no other. The true city opens up for him, myths and legends Loren has never imagined occupying the world all around him.

It changes everything.

Soriya and Loren are together again… for the first time.

The second half of the Greystone Saga starts with a murder and a promise in—